THE CROW'S NEST

THE CROW'S NEST

A Novel

Charles Parker

iUniverse, Inc.
New York Lincoln Shanghai

THE CROW'S NEST

iUniverse books may be ordered through booksellers or by contacting:

iUniverse
2021 Pine Lake Road, Suite 100
Lincoln, NE 68512
www.iuniverse.com
1-800-Authors (1-800-288-4677)

Because of the dynamic nature of the Internet, any Web addresses or links contained in this book may have changed since publication and may no longer be valid.

This is a work of fiction. All of the characters, names, incidents, organizations, and dialogue in this novel are either the products of the author's imagination or are used fictitiously.

ISBN: 978-0-595-47590-2 (pbk)
ISBN: 978-0-595-91855-3 (ebk)

Printed in the United States of America

I dedicate <u>THE CROW'S NEST</u> to my dear family, campers all, and to all those who cherish our precious Mother Earth and strive to protect it.

PREFACE

Enter the flooded and dangerous world of the year 2049 with two brave children, Will and Sara Anchor, on a mission to save their mother. The fictional world of 2049 is far different from the world today, but many scientists believe these changes may actually come to pass. The author, an engineer, is profoundly concerned about the warming and pollution of the global environment, and has chosen this fictional account to create awareness of the problem, especially for young readers. Despite the setting, the story is upbeat and life affirming, a delightful tale for all ages.

JANUARY 6, 2049
NEW ORLEANS,
LOUISIANA

My name is William Anchor, Will for short, and the time to tell this story is long overdue. As I look back at that day, January 6, 2049, it seems as if every moment, every emotion, is chiseled in my memory. Sara and I were to start out alone at daybreak the following morning in the canoe to find help for Mom. We were both thrilled and uneasy about the adventure to come!

Sara, my sister, was thirteen and destined to become a beautiful woman. I was a skinny lad of eleven and not quite sure of where my place was in the pecking order. Mom had started calling me her "man," sort of telling me to take charge, I thought, but Sara was having none of that! We were good kids and didn't quarrel, maybe because we knew how desperately we needed each other. We lived in what had been a nice part of New Orleans, the French Quarter, higher ground than most of the city, yet now flooded. The water, even on a calm day, had reached the top step of the porch and the city appeared to be completely deserted.

When we first got that canoe, Mom had pleaded with us to take it and save ourselves before the storm season began again. Poor Mom was so sick, too sick to be moved. I think maybe she wanted to die there in her pretty room full of all her framed photos of Daddy and us when we were little, but of course we could not leave her alone; it was unthinkable.

Mom fell sick about the time our Dad died and now Dad had been dead for over four months. Dad was a hero because he drowned trying to rescue one of our neighbor's children, back when we still had neighbors. Mom told us over and over about how it happened, and so many other wonderful things that Dad had done so we would have fine memories of him. Dad worked at the power plant, back when we still had electricity. He was seldom home, running the plant almost by himself after so many of the workers drowned in the hurricane of 2042, hurricane Zandra, when I was only four years old. We had seen so many storms while we were growing up that we almost got used to them and kind of took them for granted. The storm that took Dad's life, back in August, was windy and wild. It was not bad enough to have a woman's name, but it was awful nevertheless.

The reason our family stayed in the city as it began to drown was that Dad felt it was his duty to keep the power plant operating as long as possible for the hospital, and, of course, Mom wasn't about to leave him. If she had, I know that we kids would have been really devastated because we loved Dad so much, even though we saw so little of him. Dad had a cot at the plant and often he was away for a whole month. That made his visits all the more special.

Then the hospital and the power plant finally shut down so that Dad could be home to stay with us at last. He was with us for a whole week and it was so wonderful to have Daddy at home! We were all planning how to leave New Orleans using the rowboat when the weather turned suddenly violent again. Sara and I had gone to bed, and despite the howling of the wind, we were feeling confident about Daddy's plans and never knew until the morning about the tragedy that had befallen us. Daddy had drowned during the night! He had gone out in the rowboat to save a child in the water. He had apparently capsized and the child, Daddy, and the rowboat were all swept away. Dad was an excellent swimmer, but perhaps he struck his head and became unconscious.

Several of our neighbors who had boats, searched all the next day, but no sign of them could be found. It was as if lightening had struck us. I have confusing recollections of neighbors trying to help us and give us comfort, but all Sara and I felt was total despair. We had lost our Daddy! Poor Mom was so brave. She was grieving for Daddy too and beginning to be sick, but still she was trying to care for us.

After that storm, all of our neighbors left the city by whatever means they could. We were so grief stricken over the loss of Daddy that we barely noticed what was going on. That storm was the "last straw" according to Mr. Jones, who lived next door. Mrs. Jones pleaded with Mom to escape the city with them in their old powerboat. They must have had twenty people on board already, too many for safety, so Mom said we would wait for the Coast Guard to come back. The Coast Guard had been taking people to safety, load after load, for over a month, so we expected them to come for us too, but we had waited too long! The Coast Guard never came. We were abandoned!

But that was all before Kate, Mom's sister, our own Aunt Kate, arrived! Just about noon, one day early in December, we heard a loud banging on the front door and when we peeked out, there she was! You just can't imagine the excitement! Sara remembered her, but I just recognized her from pictures. Poor Mom was so happy to see her she got out of bed and would have collapsed on the floor if Kate hadn't caught her. Kate helped her to a chair then kneeled beside her and the two of them cried and hugged for the longest time. Soon Sara and I joined them in a big family "hug-in," all of us crying and laughing together. Then suddenly Aunt Kate stood up and, sounding like some sort of army sergeant, said, "Enough of this! We have work to do. Sara, get me some fresh sheets for the bed. Will …" pointing at me, "unload my rowboat!" I tackled that job with fervor, trying to imagine what might be in each sealed container, but resisted the temptation to peek.

Things changed fast after that and all for the better. All we really knew of Kate was that she lived in Ohio and was a nurse by profession. She was Mom's only living sibling. After the mail quit, phones and batteries ran out of power,

our Aunt Kate had faded from memory, my memory anyway. Every time Sara or I asked her how she found us, she
would laugh and say, "With great difficulty! I'll tell you
when we have time." She was doing great things for Mom,
so much more than Sara and I had been able to do. She had
medical and nursing skills, but maybe more than that, she
had a wonderful sense of humor. It was so great to hear
Mom laughing in her bedroom.

Finally we reached the point when Kate began to act
more like an aunt than an army sergeant. By now she knew
where to find things and daily life became more routine.
She had brought many much needed supplies in her rowboat, tea bags being one of them. So, one day when Kate
called out, "Tea time!" Sara and I came running. Mom was
sitting up in bed looking happy, so the rest of us picked up
the mood.

Kate explained that this was a "business meeting,"
which, for some reason made us, Sara and me anyway, start
giggling. Kate waited for us to get over that before she
dropped the bombshell: Sara and I, just the two of us, were
to take the canoe and try to get a rescue party for Mom.
She did not elaborate on just what was wrong with Mom
that she could not fix, but said hospital care was essential.
Kate said that she must stay with Mom, but that Sara and I
were such able young people that she and Mom both knew
we could do this task. At first the idea thrilled us, but as
Kate told us about how the world had changed, with huge
areas under water, especially in the southern half of the
United States, and of some of the scary things to beware of,

such as eddy currents, rough water and "hot" electric lines, our desire for adventure began to cool a little.

Weeks before Kate's arrival Mom had done all she could to prepare us for this canoe trip. Amazingly, one windy night, a canoe, complete with three paddles, had washed right up on our porch! We tied it fast and figured someone might come to claim it, but no one did, so we pulled it into the hall, for safekeeping. Now we had a means of escape and Mom said it was a gift from God. Now it was time for Sara and me to learn a new skill.

Sara and I knew how to handle a rowboat, but a canoe is something different. Mom had us take the canoe out on nice days and practice paddling through our flooded neighborhood until we both had the "J" stroke down pat. Mom sat in a chair on the upstairs balcony giving orders until she was satisfied we could handle all sorts of situations. Using the "clock" method to describe direction, she would shout, "One o'clock—Rock" or "Alligator—Twelve o'clock-Back-paddle" or "Garbage—Nine o'clock!" to see how fast we could maneuver the canoe.

Mom made lists of the essentials to take in the canoe: life jackets and the spare paddle, the canned food, dried food, the solar still, sun protection, rain protection, the GPS which was out of battery (but maybe we might find some) and the camera (with the same problem) and—well, you get the picture.

If and when we left on this adventure, Mom said we were to paddle north through the city not stopping to help people, if we saw any, or lost pets (we silently made no promises on that order). When we encountered open water, we were to wait until daybreak before forging ahead, so we would be able to reach the other shore in daylight; we were never to canoe in the dark! All of this was once dry land with things like telephone poles and TV antennas sticking up, nasty stuff to run into! Then there was the possibility of meeting an alligator. "Pop it hard on the nose with the edge of your paddle," said Mom, "and don't let that critter grab ya!" Mom explained that she spoke from experience on that matter. Mom and Dad had canoed and camped in Georgia on their honeymoon. They had met alligators!

Over the years Mom had told us so much about how to do things. She taught us to read and write. She taught us history, math, and geography (as it used to be). Mom was a high school teacher before the school shut down and so she home schooled Sara and me and said we were the smartest kids she ever met. She had seen a lot of kids, but Sara and I knew very few.

When it was hot, Mom put up wet towels in the windows for evaporative cooling; that worked fine if a breeze was blowing. Cooking was done in the abandoned house next door that had a wood stove. We made a bridge between our front porches to get there and we burned old furniture in the stove.

Food was mostly Army "C" rations, and sometimes canned beans or hash that Dad had scrounged up, but that is not all we had to eat. The house next door had a roof garden which our neighbor, Mrs. Jones, "willed" to us when they left. Mrs. Jones had planted a variety of vegetables along with flowers of every sort. This garden was Mom's favorite project, until climbing the stairs became too much for her. She especially liked it in the fall when the sun was less intense. In the evening it was a lovely place to sit and watch the falling stars and feel the cool breeze. Sara and I kept it weeded and watered, carrying water up three flights of stairs. We had string beans, tomatoes, squash and cabbage. Believe you me; we kids ate our veggies!

We had a three-step operation for drinking water: 1-We would scoop up the cleanest water we could see by the porch and would distill that in the solar still. This would eliminate most impurities. 2-We would boil it on the stove, making it even safer. 3-We would find some breezy spot and cool it with wet towels, using evaporation. Actually it wasn't too bad, especially as a tea.

Mom was a practical woman. According to her plan, before Kate showed up, we were to take a sealed, stamped envelope addressed to our Uncle John, Dad's brother, an attorney in New York City, to mail when and if we could, a framed photo of our family, and her hand written memoir. We were to simply leave her there in her bed. Just pack up and go! Just leave her, maybe to die, all alone? No matter how much she wanted us to leave her back then and save ourselves, we could not, and we did not. Now, thank heaven, Kate would be with her, so it was a whole different matter. Now we had a chance to save Mom's life!

JANUARY 7, 2049
SETTING OUT

Sara and I barely slept that night. I heard Sara pacing the floor, moving things in her room all night. I know because I lay awake looking at the dark watery street in the pale light of the new moon, the only light except for stars, reflecting on the water. In that light it almost looked clean and I guess it was cleaner than when there were other people in the city. Now only their ghosts were there.

Mom was lying in her bed too, with Kate's bed pulled up beside her. The very thought of Mom maybe dieing before we could get help got me crying again and I guess I was a bit noisy about it because suddenly Sara was beside me, stroking my face and telling me every thing would be all right. Sara got in beside me then and maybe we did sleep a little. Sara could be bossy, but she could be sweet too.

At first light of morning I was awakened by Sara downstairs in the kitchen with Kate preparing our breakfast of

US Army "C" rations. Dad had acquired them some time ago, but they were still edible. That, with some sun tea, would have to hold us until we knew not when or where. We had prepared for this for several days, packing and repacking over and over until we felt we had it right. The gear sat on the kitchen table and counters; every item had its assigned spot in the canoe: canned goods on the bottom, cooking kit, mountain tent and sleeping bags (used by Mom and Dad on their honeymoon) next, clothing in duffle bags, a waterproof packet of the things Mom had entrusted to our care and a tarp to be tied over all so that rain would run to the outside, not into the canoe. Lastly, on top of all and securely tied would sit the solar still and the extra paddle.

The battered 17ft. aluminum canoe, painted a brilliant yellow (Mom's idea for better visibility), rested on its side in the front hall, too wide to fit through the door leading to the porch. We would load it when we got it onto the porch. We wore hats, long sleeved shirts and long pants, for protection from the sun. And we both had leather gloves to keep our hands from getting blisters. Mom was an expert canoe handler, so we trusted her advice. Sara and I both knew the "J" stroke so we could switch places if needed. Mom suggested that Sara paddle stern on the first day, however, and I felt a little put down by that, as I recall. My job as bowman, was to paddle hard on whichever side Sara told me and watch carefully for hidden debris. Sara had a street map of New Orleans as a guide and she would do the steering.

With breakfast done we made one last check of the house. I was glad to see Sara pick up her favorite doll making it OK for me to grab my teddy bear. It was clear we were not quite ready for adulthood. We closed the windows, I'm not sure why. We each took a turn in the upstairs bathroom. Flushing the toilet required a trip to the porch for a pail of water, but amazingly it always flushed, but to where we preferred not to think.

Mom looked all sweet and pretty, sitting up in bed. We said our goodbyes kind of fast so as not to start crying our eyes out, and promised to take all the precautions they had drilled into us. Getting the canoe onto the porch was easy enough and loading was automatic, after all the drills. Kate was there to help slide the canoe into the water. Before we climbed in she gave each of us a really vigorous kiss and whispered how proud she was of us. Poor Aunt Kate was crying now, wondering, perhaps, if she was doing the right thing to send us kids off into the unknown.

Finally, ready and in our places, I tucked my teddy under the belt of my life jacket, so he could help me navigate, and gave the all clear. The canoe responded slowly to our paddling at first, being heavily loaded, but once in motion it was easy to hold our course and glided smoothly down the street, our street, our canal. I could hear Sara behind me. She was sobbing, but she managed to give me a clear message from our dear Daddy, quoting an expression he often said, "Don't look back!" Ah, but I did, and there stood Kate waving with both arms! I stopped paddling to wave back, and Sara shouted, "PADDLE!"

Neither of us spoke for a while and when we did it felt as if we should whisper. This was a part of the city we knew well and now it was dead. There must have been ghosts about because I could feel them, but knowing what Sara would say, I kept this to myself. Sara said ghosts were only make-believe. The homes here were so beautiful once, with fancy iron railings on second floor verandas, and French windows, and in a sad way, they were still beautiful in death.

I couldn't see Sara, because she was behind me, but I was sure she was crying. There were children that used to live here only a few months before. We used to wave to each other and I knew several by name, but I never knew them well. Now they had all left, along with their families, in the rescue boats, so I would probably never see them again. It made me feel so empty inside, so alone. I suspect Sara felt that way too.

On and on we went, moving fast in the calm water. The sun was shining on the tops of the buildings now, but had not reached us yet in the watery canyons, so we were still relatively cool. Kate had made sure we got an early start. It was shaping up to be a nice winter day, hot but bearable. I had my shirt off now, but Sara, being a girl, had to keep hers on. I felt sorry for her and told her so, but she said I should save my pity for my arm muscles and to keep paddling.

After about an hour we reached Lake Pontchartrain with row after row of what were once fancy hotels. The lake was huge, at least to us, and too rough for us to attempt, so we went toward the west, staying a block or two away from the shoreline, behind the front row of buildings. Our plan, actually the plan Mom laid out on the map for us, was to follow the western shore then keep heading north. If we went north far enough, Mom figured we would find people living on dry land, with cars and everything the way people used to live. We hoped she was right.

It was about this time that Sara had a great idea. If we could find a safe looking hotel to go into and climb the stairs to the top, we could see a long ways and better plan our route. Besides that, we needed a rest stop since paddling was really hard now. The first building we tried had its doors firmly locked, as did the second and third. At the forth hotel our luck was good. Not only was the door unlocked, it was wide open, so we could paddle right into the foyer with water about a foot deep. As we came in a whole flock of birds flew out, which made Sara squeal in shock. I was cool and never made a sound.

For awhile we just sat there looking around at what used to be a beautiful room. There definitely were ghosts in there. We drifted up to the grand staircase and I tied us fast to the balustrade. Sara got out the binoculars and off we went, glad to be using our legs instead of our arms for a change. The stairs on this first section were wide with red carpeting, torn in spots. The remaining stairs were in a plain stairwell, with doors to enter each floor. When we reached the sixth and final door we entered what was once a restaurant or nightclub with large windows, several of them broken out, looking out over Lake Pontchartrain. What a sight! Sara had the first look with the binoculars and said that even with them she could barely make out anything on the far shore of the lake. When my turn came I could do no better. It was a very heart-stopping sight; water as far as the eye could see. Looking westward was more encouraging because there were buildings: even with watery streets, they were more comforting to look at.

There was no place to sit down that was not covered with bird droppings, so we went down to the floor below and checked to see what the rooms were like. To our surprise, the first room we peeked into, other than smelling a bit musty, looked great, beds all made up, towels in the bath, the works. The windows were dirty, but intact, so no bird "do". We closed the door, each picked a bed and stretched out for a nap. Oh how nice it was to feel like royalty in that spotlessly clean room, made up for us by a maid years before! Soon we were fast asleep.

JANUARY 8, 2049
THE HOTEL

We must have been more tired than we realized because when we woke, both at the same time, it was pitch dark outside and it was raining hard. I think it was thunder that woke us and now it was the occasional flashes of lightening that gave us light to see by since the starlight was hidden. Sara came to sit with me and put her arm around my shoulders. It was an awesome sight to see lightening across open water. It was comforting to feel so well protected and Sara reminded me about what Mom would say about God taking care of us. I suppose she was right.

Sara had a watch, one of the wind-up kind that once belonged to our grandpa, Dad's father. She was careful to keep it wound and it told us that we had slept a very long time, well past midnight! All our food was in the canoe, and we were as hungry as bears, so off we went feeling our way slowly down the stair well and then the grand staircase. We could hear the canoe gently bumping against the stair. Then we detected another sound, a low rumbling sound, that stopped us from moving forward. I guess Sara was braver than I because she said in a low voice, "Is someone there?"

As if in answer there was a brilliant flash of lightening and a terrible boom of thunder at the same instant. (I think our hotel must have been hit.) There, sitting in the middle of our canoe tarp, clearly illuminated by the lightening, sat a large white cat, looking as if it were waiting there for us, expecting us. Suddenly it was there beside us, rubbing hard against my leg and purring a message of gratitude and friendship. Oh, what a love fest ensued after that, with all the hugging and petting. Now we had a friend to travel with us and share our adventure. We were so happy we nearly forgot about food. A name, we needed a name. "Snowball" seemed just right, even though neither Sara nor I had ever seen snow. Sara said she knew for certain that Snowball was a girl, but she wouldn't tell me how she knew.

Now we turned to food, hoping our new friend would like Army "C" rations. With food in hand and some clean water from the still the three of us climbed the stairs again to the bedroom we had adopted. Snowball liked it just fine, especially the pillow on my bed. Soon we were all eating cold "C" rations there on the floor. The rain had stopped and there was now a faint light on the eastern horizon. Surprisingly, Snowball was not very hungry, and feeling her tummy, she felt well fed. She was obviously a pet in former years and had fed well on birds and rodents. Now she had what all cats and humans need: companionship and love.

That morning we got a really early start. I took the bow so as not to have an argument in front of Snowball. She, Snowball, sat on her tarp as she had the night before, and Sara said calming things to her as the canoe moved away from the staircase because she did look somewhat alarmed; this may have been her first canoe ride. As we paddled out and down the street Snowball sat up very straight and alert, taking in the sights. Sara said she wished she could tell us about all the things she had seen and where she had been, but we comforted ourselves by the knowledge that her story would be our story from here on.

The water was calm and the air fresh after the rain. We were feeling great too, so the buildings flew by block after block. Now Sara started to talk to Snowball as if she could understand everything she said. I don't know why, but this started to get to me after awhile. Then came the time she shifted sides with her paddle and dripped a couple of drops of water on Snowball and was SO apologetic. Never was she that considerate of me. Suddenly I was so mad I just stopped paddling, and I told her why too! She stopped too, saying nothing, waiting until I simmered down. Then, to my surprise, Snowball came around from behind me and placed herself firmly on my lap. She knew how to quell an argument and proved to me that she understood the emotion, if not the words I was saying. She wanted love and harmony. I sat there petting Snowball for awhile until I was able to put my apology to Sara into words. Strange how silly little things can make us mad and spoil our day. Things went smoothly after that.

Before long as we traveled our route one or two blocks from shore, we could tell by the sun that we were no longer going west, but starting to go north and we could see another lake to our left, Lake Maurepas, according to our street map. The space between lakes looked to be only a couple miles wide, only the tops of buildings visible. This was one of the major benchmarks on our journey, the place we turned north. Mom and Kate had both said we were sure to reach dry land if we just kept going north from here, if not in Louisiana, then certainly in Mississippi. Since our map only covered New Orleans, not the entire state of Louisiana, we had a limited concept of how far this might be. If we had known we might have faltered in our resolve. Fortunately, we did not predict the future and just kept on going.

After several hours of hard paddling we needed a rest. We had experienced a number of close calls, almost hitting submerged cars and other junk close to the surface. The large buildings were mostly behind us now, and the homes poorer; many were nothing but debris of homes never rebuilt after all the storms. We were looking for a solid looking porch to sit on and finally a warehouse came into view with a concrete loading dock a few inches above the water. It seemed perfect until we got close and we were greeted with a sickening smell, something chemical, that kept us moving on as fast as possible. Snowball had noticed the smell first, making guttural sounds to warn us, and I'm sure she was thinking, "Can't humans smell anything?"

Well, it wasn't quite what we were looking for, but we tied up to a tree, or rather the trunk of a tree, in what appeared to be a park, all of the trees just broken remnants. Snowball approved of this place and immediately scampered up to the top, about ten feet, perhaps looking in the hollow to find a bird for lunch. The water was shallow so we rolled up our pants and stepped out. It felt great to stretch our legs, but we soon got back in the canoe when we thought how easily alligators could hide among the fallen limbs all around us. We opened a "C" ration and had lunch, with Snowball looking down at us, apparently not interested in what we were eating; we were pretty sick of it ourselves. She had bird on her mind.

We had to rest, but we couldn't do it there, so we untied the canoe, called Snowball (she already knew her name) and pressed on, looking for a building to rest in. This was a region that had been hit hard by storms and few structures were still standing. After several miles of this we spotted a small white Baptist church sitting a bit above water line on one of the muddy little islands that now dotted the landscape. It was just what we needed because another storm seemed to be gathering in the east. We slid the old yellow canoe up on the bank and set off to explore our new haven.

Well, the inside had seen a lot of water in the past and smelled very musty, but our standards were pretty low by this time so we prepared to stay. We had managed to tie the canoe to the church sign and had taken in food and the sleeping bags, and were headed back out for another load, when what should appear from around the corner of the church but a huge, at least ten feet long, alligator! He was moving fast, right toward us! Sara screamed, and it was good she did. With Snowball in the lead we all managed to beat him to the door and slam it in his face. As Mom would have said, "God was with you again, and don't you forget it!"

We figured that we had all that we really needed from the canoe, considering the monster waiting at our door, so we each picked a pew and rolled out a sleeping bag to lie on top of. This time Snowball chose me to be her sleeping buddy and it was the first time in years that I didn't need my teddy bear. It soon began raining hard, but this was a sound building with a good roof. We were very fortunate children to have found this place and like the afternoon and night before, we were so tired that we slept right on through to daybreak.

JANUARY 9, 2049
THE BAPTIST
CHURCH

As usual, Sara was the first one up. She had managed to start a small fire in the wood stove, which sat in the central area of the room. We did not need the heat, but "C" rations were better when heated. This time Snowball agreed to eat with us. The rain had stopped, but the sky looked like more rain might come. When we looked out a small window at the front we were glad to see that the gator was nowhere in sight, but when we opened the door and peeked out, there he was waiting for us by the canoe! We were stuck! Well, the weather settled our problem for the time being because it suddenly was raining hard again.

Now, Sara and I had lived much of our young lives housebound enduring such conditions. We had our own games, some of our own invention, some from Mom and

Dad. In our beautiful New Orleans home we kept our bod-
ies strong by racing each other up the stairs (never down),
doing push-ups and chin-ups. One large room had been
emptied out so we could have a gym. We had grand soccer
games there, often with Mom, and sometimes Dad, in the
cheering section. So on this rainy day in the church we just
hunkered down to wait out that alligator. We assumed he
would sooner or later go off on some other alligator pur-
suit. In our young minds, we both felt pretty cocky about
our ability to out-run him if it came down to a chase.

JANUARY 11, 2049
THE TREE HOUSE

The rain came down all day, and the next day as well. Finally, on January 11th, when our patience had really worn thin, the sun rose in a clear cloudless sky and we knew it was time to go. Peeking out the rear door that faced east, we spotted our enemy. He was basking in the sun, apparently sound asleep. The canoe was out at the front, tied to the sign. Sara told me to keep an eye on the gator while she got the canoe loaded and ready to go. If the gator began to move toward her I was to shout a warning.

It went almost according to plan. Sara quietly loaded the canoe, untied it and pushed it to the waters edge, while I held Snowball and watched at the back door. When Sara tapped me on the shoulder and said it was ready, I carefully closed the back door and we left by the front door thinking we were safe. Just when we were half way to the waters edge, that monster came roaring around the corner and the only escape was to keep running and hopefully out-run that critter. Snowball had been in my arms as we left the church, but she leapt down to run on her own when the gator appeared; now she led the way. She was one fast cat!

We ran all the way around the church with the alligator at our heels. The ground was muddy and slippery after all that rain, making it better for the alligator and worse for us! We could hear him breathing and he seemed to be gaining on us, but I didn't dare look back to see, for fear I might trip and fall. The very thought of being eaten alive gives one strength to move fast!

As we rounded the last corner, I heard Sara say, "Canoe" so that is where we headed. When we got there we pushed off and leapt in, sort of like an Olympic toboggan team. Snowball landed, legs spread wide, claws extended, gripping the tarp for dear life. We didn't dare look back to check on our enemy until we were in the canoe and paddling wildly away. We were totally out of breath.

Finally, looking back, we saw the alligator, appearing disinterested, bored really, stretched out enjoying the sun. He had stopped chasing us about thirty feet from the water's edge! As I recall that chase, I think he might have caught us if he had kept coming. We knew just what Mom would have said, something like, "God saved your lives again. I hope you noticed!" Yes indeed, Mom, we sure did notice!

Well, after the excitement of having escaped death inside that gator we felt as if nothing could stop us from here on. The rain of the last couple days had made the little islands disappear. Except for the tops of telephone poles and some rooftops, very little stuck above the surface. If we looked back over our right shoulder we could still make out the taller buildings of New Orleans. Sara said, "Don't look back! Keep paddling!" I told her I wanted a turn at paddling stern and she said I could after we took our next rest stop. Looking at all the open water ahead I wondered when that might happen.

Except for the aching in my arms, things went pretty well for a long time. There was a steady breeze, sometimes quite hard, at our back keeping us cool and pushing us along. We had well over a hundred miles to go to reach the higher ground that Mom told us we were sure to find in Mississippi, the lower end of a mountain range, the Appalachians, extending all the way up to Maine. This was certain to be inhabited, in fact, probably crowded, with people who were displaced by the new global water table.

To think that anyone could ever question the changes that would come with global warming! Back then as an eleven-year-old boy I had little knowledge of what life was like in our grandparent's day, except for stories Mom and Dad told us. It was not as if people were not warned. They were amply warned, but those in charge, those in Washington, were apparently incapable of making the meaningful changes necessary to avoid a disaster. Ah, but I have digressed from my story. Back to the year 2049!

We were approaching the State of Mississippi at a pretty good clip now. The reason we were making such good time was a kind of sail that Sara rigged up using the tarp, still tied down at the front end, but tied to the spare paddle and lifted high by Sara using her paddle held upright. Snowball curled up at Sara's feet. It was now up to me to steer as best

I could from the bow end, and I soon got the hang of it. Boy, how we moved, and best of all it was easier on our arms. The sail had been my idea so it was about then that Sara paid me one of those rare compliments, telling me she thought I was a genius! I told her that she was pretty smart too.

One small problem was that Sara had trouble seeing where we were going, with the tarp blocking her vision. Also, around mid-day it was hard to predict our compass heading, (not having a compass), using the sun location as our guide. On the good side there were few things to run into in this open expanse of water. We weren't sure where we were going, but we were getting there fast!

I don't know how I missed it, but I did. Suddenly, with a screech, we came to a sudden stop on the metal roof of a building just below the surface of the water. Sara lowered the sail and we just sat awhile thinking and studying the horizon with the binoculars. Looking slightly to the right of where the wind was taking us we both saw something, maybe land, maybe a mirage, but now we had a sighting to aim toward.

Sara checked her watch. It was about noon so we lunched right there in the canoe. I was eager to change our seating position and stepped out of the canoe onto the sloped, and very slippery, roof. Big mistake! Down I went, nearly tipping the canoe over. In my struggles to get up, I splashed water on Snowball and what she told me was not fit to print! Sara then moved gracefully up to the bow, keeping her body low, hands on the gunnels, then steadied the canoe with her paddle while I got back in. I felt a bit foolish, but oh how nice and cool the water felt evaporating off my back.

This time we rigged the sail with a rope attached to the right end, the "starboard" end according to my know-it-all sister. I was to pull on that rope and hold up the sail at the same time so we could "tack." Her only job was to sit up front holding Snowball and tell me how hard to pull because she was the "navigator." Well I couldn't complain because I had asked to be back there. I did feel as if I had been snookered into something, despite the obvious fact that this was far easier than paddling.

After maybe three hours of this Sara said she was now sure we were headed for dry land and there were buildings too, but not a lot of big ones. We had a few close calls with debris in the water, but she was able to keep us out of trouble with her paddle. She was leaning back in her seat now so that her back was helping support the mast-paddle. She really could be a good sister, as well as being a smarty-pants.

Suddenly Sara shouted, "Lower the sail!" and when I did, I could see why. Coming up fast was an obstruction, barely below the surface, that might have turned us over. Now with both of us back paddling against the wind and our momentum, we gently came up to it and found that it was a train, tipped on its side, the word "Amtrak" visible through the murky water. What an awesome sight! This was a passenger train. Were there people down there? The thought sent chills up my spine! Just below us there were windows we might have peered into, but Sara ordered me not to look.

The train was lying across our path so we had to paddle hard against the wind to eventually get around it. When we did, we continued to use our paddles, instead of the sail, so that we would have better control in case there were more things that might snare us. The water was shallow now and we found ourselves in the midst of numerous tiny islands, barely above the water, some with deserted buildings. This is what we had thought might be the high ground we were seeking. As we had recently learned this was just the place that alligators love, a place to sun themselves after swimming, so we kept on going, despite the fact that we were bone tired and the sun was getting low in the sky

Eventually one little island caught our attention and we decided to investigate. One large tree dominated the area and in it we could see a tree house, apparently in good shape. On the ground nearby were the remnants of a large house that had burned down. Nice people with children had once lived here, so, setting aside our gator fears, we scuffed ashore, and raced to claim our prize.

Sara was first to climb up, inspecting each rung of the ladder to be sure it was safe. The ladder took us to a small porch with a handrail about fifteen feet above the ground. Behind that was a walled in room, about six feet square, with a window opening in each wall and a roof with a wide overhang, that appeared to be sound. Headroom inside was fine for us, but an adult would need to bend over. It was perfect! Snowball gave it a thorough inspection and liked it too.

We lost no time securing the canoe and settling into our new quarters. There was a rope attached to the handrail for hauling up sleeping bags and such. Just inside the door stood a broom, child size, that Sara placed in my hand and said, "Get to work!" Aside from a few leaves, the floor was actually quite clean, despite the presence of numerous birds in the tree above us. Seems that smart birds prefer trees to buildings any day. And the tree above us, all around us, was simply gorgeous. There was no sign of lightening strike and as we looked further, we found out why. The tree was wired with a lightening rod to the ground. That's what I call going the "extra mile" to protect your children!

At the end of the porch there was still another ladder that went much higher in the tree to a little seat near the top. Oh, it was tempting, but we were so tired we postponed that climb until morning. Instead, we ate a cold supper of canned salmon and canned peaches, a special treat that Mom had insisted we take along. There was just room enough for the two of us to sit cross-legged there on our porch, with Snowball sitting between us. We had already opened out our sleeping bags, side-by-side in the main room in preparation for bedtime. So there we sat, cross-legged, passing the salmon can back and forth and dishing out a share for Snowball. The porch faced west, providing a perfect spot to view the sunset. The sun was orange and huge as it sank below the horizon and it made the expanse of water seem to be on fire. It was simply breathtaking!

Then suddenly, as if a conductor had tapped his baton, the birds began to sing like never before. There seemed to be hundreds of them, all twittering love ballads above us.

Sara looked at me grinning. "This is heaven, Will, I think we've found heaven!" she said. "If only Mom were here."

"Mom isn't, but maybe Daddy is." I replied.

"Maybe—no, more than maybe. I can feel him right here, Will, I feel sure of it. Do you feel it too?" she asked.

I nodded and we both sat very still letting the warmth of that longing fill our hearts. I was glad that Sara, who claimed never to believe in ghosts, could nevertheless feel Dad's presence. That made me feel closer to Sara and I reached over and held her hand. I really did love my smarty-pants sister.

Ever since leaving Mom and Kate in New Orleans, Sara and I had said very little to each other, maybe because we were so occupied in the work of paddling, the business of surviving, that meaningful communication took a back seat. Now, finally, we were at ease and feeling happy, so the floodgates began to open. All those things we had been keeping to ourselves began to come out. We talked and talked far into the night, lying on top of our sleeping bags now. We had been so tired, physically, at the start of the evening; now we were jabbering away like a couple of kids. We had finally found each other!

JANUARY 12, 2049
HIGH GROUND

When I awoke the next morning to the sound of birds twittering and Sara moving about, I just called out to the world in general, "I want to live here the rest of my life!"

"Sorry, Will, I need you to help paddle," she said. "I just took a look from the treetop with the binoculars and we still have a long way to go. It looks like open water after we pass this bunch of islands and the wind is with us again. So, up an' at 'em! That means you too, Snowball!"

She was right; we had to get a move on. So despite Snowball's grumbling and my sluggishness, we had a quick breakfast, left our lovely tree house and shoved off. I was rather slow getting my paddle in the water because I wanted to have a last look at our lovely abode. Sara, acting bossy again, felt compelled to quote Dad once more, shouting, "Don't look back!"

Well, this day went like clockwork because we had a strong wind, stronger than the day before, and we had the sail control down pat. We got an early start, it was still cool, and we felt quite sure of our direction, so the water just flew by. We did have a few close calls with floating tree limbs and such, but the dangers we feared most, of things just below the surface seemed to be behind us for the time being. I am sure the actual water depth was not over 10 feet, maybe much less, but the impression we had was of traversing a vast ocean; no land in sight. It was both scary and thrilling. I began to fantasize that perhaps we were the very last people on Earth.

It was very fortunate for us that the wind was steady instead of gusting. Sara calculated that the direction of the wind was about 15 degrees off our course so we sat close to the starboard edge to keep the canoe from going over. It was a very delicate balance and more than once we came close to capsizing. I was bowman again. I had the binoculars trained on a speck in the distance that I hoped was dry land and I relayed instructions to Sara who controlled the sail rope with one hand and the rudder paddle with the other.

We were so intensely occupied that it was mid-afternoon before we began to feel the pangs of hunger. By this time the speck I had been aiming for had become much bigger and now we felt certain that we were headed in the right direction. It was time to celebrate so we dropped the sail in order to eat a well-deserved lunch, letting the wind push us at will.

Almost as if it were a sign from heaven, a sudden squall hit us. The sun was still shining brightly off to the west, while rain in huge drops poured down! Sara spread the canvas over our gear and Snowball lost no time finding a dry spot underneath. Actually the rain felt good, but the scary part was how the water suddenly became very rough. With lunch forgotten, we began to paddle hard to keep the canoe headed into the waves, since getting sideways in rough water could swamp us. This took us somewhat off course, but after about half an hour of hard paddling, the rain stopped along with the wind. Soon the water became calmer and it was time to get back on course. Sara tried the sail again, but now the weather had changed and there was so little breeze that we gave that up in favor of paddling.

The thought that we were so close to our goal of finding people, real live people, people who might help save Mom and Aunt Kate, gave us such a charge of energy that it felt good to work those tired arms again. Even without the binoculars we could now see low buildings, many of them, very close together seeming to completely cover the base of the low hills that rose from the water's edge.

The water here was shallow and filled with debris of all kinds, foul smelling debris. The closer we got to shore the worse it seemed to be. More than once we had to back-paddle to avoid something just inches below the surface. It was slow going compared to our recent sailing before the wind. Now the air was still, barely moving, and the sun had dropped behind the hills on shore, making the scene seem dark and foreboding. No people were visible as yet, no sign of life appeared on the shore or between the buildings. Perhaps our journey had all been in vain!

Half an hour later we scuffed ashore on a muddy beach and pulled the canoe to what seemed a safe spot. Sara, carrying Snowball, led the way, climbing an embankment to a macadam roadway. The buildings bordering this road showed the same signs of storm damage we were only too familiar with. It was clear that those who once lived here had moved to higher ground, and since the land rose up quite sharply, we were sure we might still find someone there. It was laid out as a small town, the side streets climbing the hillside for a short distance until the incline became too large. Finally, with darkness approaching and feeling very tired, we started back to the canoe for supplies, planning to adopt one of the better-looking houses for the night.

We had gotten the things we needed and secured the tarp, when I stopped to look at the hill ahead of us. It was a sight that Sara and I had seldom seen, except in photographs, and now framed against the sky in deepening shadow it was awesome and frightening. It was good that it held our attention, because as we entered one of the side streets we saw a tiny light high above us, which we might not have seen otherwise. For a little while we stood there breathless, making sure it was not our imagination. It was real! There were people living up there and now we set off in earnest to find them.

One of the streets just had to go on up the hill, but finding it was not easy. It was at the far end of town and was a continuation of the main street and it seemed to head in the wrong direction, but something told us to keep going. Fortunately for us, the moon appeared from behind the clouds so we could see where we were walking. (Mom had warned us about snakes liking warm pavement.)

As we climbed further the light we had seen disappeared, and it seemed to us that we were going farther away at every step, so we sat down on our sleeping bags to rethink our plan. My sturdy legs no longer felt so sturdy. I was bone tired and ready to go to sleep right there, but Sara said, "no way." So after a brief rest we pressed on and to our delight came to a side road heading steeply up the hill in the direction, it seemed, where the light had been. There was even a small sign that read, "THE CROW'S NEST"! Off we went to find it!

THE CROW'S NEST, MISSISSIPPI

The road, more like a driveway, wound steeply up the slope in a series of switchbacks, eventually leveling off on a tranquil expanse of farmland bordered by post and rail fencing and large trees, all with heavy cables anchoring them to the ground. In the distance we could make out what appeared to be barns and sheds. The moon was high by this time giving us a clear picture of the landscape. This was a paradise quite foreign to our eyes. Snowball who had long since opted to ride atop Sara's backpack began to purr loudly; this was a place she approved of!

The road took us for some distance alongside the fencing, finally veering off toward a group of large trees. It was not until we were actually there that we saw the house. It was large, but not in the grand southern style of the French Quarter, but rather in a low rambling design. The walls were of fieldstone, giving the whole structure a very sturdy, very elegant look. If this were the source of the light we had followed, it was no longer burning, however. No matter! We had found living people at last, and Snowball's constant purring assured us of that.

We were slowly approaching a heavy front door with wrought iron hinges. We were feeling a bit timid now, when suddenly an electric light came on beside the door. The shock caused us both to freeze and Snowball to take off like a shot. When we got our wits about us, we saw a tall grey-haired man with a neatly trimmed grey beard and a friendly smile on his face, standing in the doorway. Then in a deep pleasant voice, he said, "Well, well, this is my lucky day. Visitors, and from many miles away it looks to me. Do come in and rest yourselves, enjoy some food from my pantry, tell me your names and tell me about your adventures. My name is Paul McMaster, by the way, but just call me Paul."

We were so speechless I am afraid we may have forgotten to thank him, but we eagerly entered his home, followed immediately by Snowball, who had changed her mind and returned to join us. Sara removed her pack and muddy shoes by the entrance, so, following her example, I did the same. Then, following our host, we entered a large living area furnished with beautiful braided rugs and comfortable furniture. My eyes must have been bulging because it was like entering a palace.

The first thing I did was ask to use the bathroom. The toilet was a composting toilet, the first I'd ever seen. It was odorless and used no water. There was real toilet paper. There was soap at the sink, and water came from the faucet;

so, after using the toilet, I washed my face and hands and dried on the towel that was hanging beside it. When I left the bathroom I saw that the kitchen was close by, so I timidly walked in and looked around. In the kitchen there was a refrigerator. I peeked in and found that it was cold! After I had closed the door, I looked up to see Paul standing at the kitchen door, smiling, apparently amused at my childish behavior.

That emboldened me to go about turning on lights. At that, however, Paul stopped me. He had solar power, he said, and explained that this charged batteries, and only a few things could be turned on at one time. I felt rather ashamed of myself after that, and Sara was looking daggers at me, but Paul acted as if it were nothing at all.

"Let's start with something to eat," he said. "What would you like? I have bread and butter and jam from our berry patch. The butter is goat butter, and I have nice cold goat milk too. How does that sound for starters?" When he found out we had been eating an almost constant diet of Army "C" Rations, he advised us to go light at first so our stomachs could get used to the change. We sat at a table in the kitchen thoroughly enjoying several large slices of the delicious bread and jam. The milk tasted good, but it was strange to us, since we had seldom tasted cow's milk, let alone that from a goat. While we ate, our host used the time to wash a few dishes at the sink, before sitting down with us. He said that he had already had his supper, but kept offering us more choices from his larder. We kept thanking him and saying we were full, even though we really might have enjoyed more. We were trying hard to be polite, and the warm expression in Paul's eyes told me we were making a good impression.

Finally, with clean hands and supper done, we sat down together in the living room to become better acquainted. To make it official, Snowball hopped down out of my lap and into Paul's. Sara did most of the talking now, explaining what our mission was, to get help for Mom, and a brief review of what we had been through. All the while, Paul sat across from us, totally absorbed in our tale, asking questions and making comments. He wanted to know all about Mom and our Aunt Kate, and about what Daddy did before he died. Paul said it was truly astounding that we had come so far by canoe.

Then I spoke up, "Why is this called the Crow's Nest? Do you have a lot of crows?"

"Good question," he replied, "Some crows do stop by here, especially after seed planting, but the real reason is this. When my wife, Emily, and I built this estate years ago, she said the view up here was like being in the crow's nest of a sailing ship, a seat for a lookout high up on the mast. We both liked the name, so it stuck. Unfortunately, my Emily is no longer here to enjoy the view. Emily passed away nearly ten years ago."

"I'm so sorry," said Sara.

"I am too," I said, in a subdued voice.

"Thank you," he replied. "Now let's get you two to bed. You must be terribly tired, so I'll show you to your rooms. Tomorrow you can continue this amazing story, because I want to know everything that happened," he said. Then he placed Snowball gently on the floor and led us to two bedrooms where he told us we could sleep as long as we wished. He also said we should both take a shower first, but not to use more water than necessary. The water, he explained, was rainwater collected in a cistern and would be warm from the sun. We were his guests for as long as we wished to be, he said, and in the morning he would look into what could be done to save our mother and aunt. Lastly, he said that if we slept late he would be working in the garden so we should come out and find him. This time we both thanked him profusely for his hospitality and gave him a hug. When he stepped back I could see tears standing in his eyes.

We were both bone-tired after our long day, but did as our host requested and took a shower before crawling between those lovely clean sheets for the night. We each had our own bedroom, beautifully furnished, with a window overlooking the expanse of water we had so recently been on. The air felt fresh and cool, due to the elevation, and I was soon off in blissful sleep.

JANUARY 13, 2049
THE HISTORY
LESSON

When I awoke in the morning it was because Snowball had jumped on top of me and began making little growling sounds in her throat. "Get up," she was saying very plainly! She had apparently done the same thing to Sara, because my sister appeared in the doorway now, laughing at us. Oh, what a beautiful thing it was, to hear my sister laugh again.

Well, it was rather late in the morning: ten o'clock by Sara's watch. The house was quiet so we left to find our new friend in the garden. Leaving the shade of the trees we were surprised to see, not only Paul, but also a great crowd of people, all working at various tasks such as picking or hoeing in a huge vegetable garden. Someone must have seen us and spoken to Paul, because he immediately straightened up and waved to us to come join them. This we did, and when we got close everyone stopped work and gathered around to greet us, with Paul doing the introductions.

In a rather booming voice, Paul introduced each person with a first name and a title, such as "The Plumber" or "The Baker." Then to us he said he could see we were puzzled by so much information all at once, so he asked one young woman, whom he referred to as Mona, "The Historian," to explain what their community was all about. Mona, in turn said, "Great idea! Let's take a break under the trees."

After everyone had taken a drink from an outside water fountain and settled on the grass she began by saying that Paul had told them all about the life we had led in New Orleans and the wild canoe adventure we had experienced getting here. (They all indicated that they were impressed.) Then she explained that their community came about as an aftermath of the devastating storm of 2042, hurricane Zandra, the terrible one that Dad had described to us. She said that Dr. Paul McMaster and his wife, who was no longer living, had built this beautiful estate long before the storm and when the waters rose rapidly worldwide, the McMasters gave them all a safe haven. Now they lived as one large family, only a small portion of which was sitting with us. She said there were about 120 people in all, and that this was about the greatest number this land area could support. When it became an island, as the water rose, they were isolated from people on the high land further north, the Appalachian Mountain Range.

Then Mona explained events that occurred worldwide because of global warming, some of which even far-sighted people like the famous US vice-president, Al Gore, did not anticipate. Dr. McMaster, she said, was a research scientist who recognized an even greater danger, but was considered an alarmist for his predictions. Mona was one of his lab assistants back then, but despite the clear signs, no one in the Washington establishment, or elsewhere in the world, would listen. Now it was too late; land-masses had sunk.

Beginning around the year 2010 the concept of utilizing the heat of the molten magma deep within the earth as a means of boiling water (to create steam to turn turbines) for power generation became very popular in most of the civilized countries. It was touted as the answer to the threat of global warming since nothing harmful was emitted into the air. But, as Paul had warned, it was soon to be our undoing!

As coal-burning plants were shut down, geothermal plants replaced them. A new means of construction had been developed, the Holondorf method, so that they were simple and inexpensive to build. Since these plants supplied a uniform flow of energy, they soon replaced windmills and other "green" energy sources.

The greatest boost to the Holondorf plants came from the world's love of the automobile. The global warming alert had resulted in a worldwide ban on burning fossil fuels of any kind, except in aircraft. This mandate resulted in a huge surge of demand for electrically charged cars and trucks throughout the world, plus all the other devices that use electricity. Third world countries were "helped" by the richer nations to "power up," even when they could ill afford to do it, to increase demand for the expensive products of the industrialized nations. Soon localized Holondorf plants were everywhere, several million covering the face of the earth; the never-ending thirst for power was drawing heat from the interior of the earth.

Scientific studies showed that air quality was improved, and that global warming had been slowed. The economies of the industrialized nations were booming, but despite all that, the earth was in deep trouble. The rising water from the melting of glaciers and the resulting flooding of coastal areas that Mr. Gore had warned of were bad, causing widespread dislocation of people in coastal regions. Now, due to the exposure of the magma to so much water, the earth was cooling internally and consequently the core of the earth was shrinking. As Paul predicted, landmasses thus began to fall and water levels to rise to levels that far exceeded our worst nightmares. In some cases the drop was sudden involving terrible earthquakes, in other cases it was a gentle lowering of the land, and in still others nothing happened, apparently creating huge voids under the landmass.

Cities, which are often near to the coastline, were hit hardest. All low-lying sections of roadway were now under water, hopelessly disrupting highway transportation. The same was true of trains. Soon the entire country was shut down: no fuel trucks or trains, no mail, no California fruit, no new stock in stores. Plane travel, except in a few rare instances, was shut down for lack of fuel. Life as we knew it had ground to a halt. People everywhere, those that survived the earthquakes and the tsunamis and those who reached high ground and a safe place to settle were forced, as were our early ancestors, to find ways to live off the land.

"We've had it pretty easy here, having our dear friend, Paul, to help us," said Mona. I noticed that Paul and most of the others had left the group, having completed their break and were off in the field again. "Hey! I bet you two are hungry, I know I am. Let's eat," she said. Then, walking into Paul's house and right into the kitchen and opening the refrigerator, she began to make us a sandwich. We must have looked a little shocked that she did this without permission from Paul, because she read my mind precisely. "You are wondering why I walk into someone else's house like this as if it were mine," she said. "That means you were well brought up. Any place else it would be wrong, but here it is what Paul wants us to do. We're all one big family. Everyone has pledged whatever he or she has to the use of all. We all have something to give, some skill to use, a better idea, an ability to knit, medical skills, maybe only a pleasant smile and a sense of humor. We all do what we can. Paul, since he began with more, can now contribute more, and that is his wish. The rest of us owe our very lives to Paul so, of course, we want to do what we can, too."

Throughout this entire lecture by Mona, we just sat there wide-eyed and speechless. Finally, Sara ventured a timid question. "We have money with us that Mom gave us. Can we give that to Paul so we can do our part?" she asked.

"Thank you, dear one, but no. There are other ways you can help. There may be some places on earth where money still has value, so hold on to it, but it has no value here. I know there are other communities further north that use the barter system, that's where you give something you have for something you don't have, but if you are destitute you have nothing to barter with. Paul wants all of us to have an equal chance for a good life no matter how much we have when we come here, so we pool our resources, therefore we all do have an equal chance. That is a better way."

Just then Paul walked into the room and sat down at the table. "Have you been talking the ears off these kids, Mona? They look positively worn out. Your lectures do go on a bit you know! Let's find out if they understood what you told them." Now turning to me, he said, "What caused the earth to shrink?"

"All the cold water hitting the earth's molten magma in so many places all over the place in order to make steam to run turbines made it cool down, the magma I mean, so it shrinks but the amount of water is still the same even though it seems to be bigger." All this I blurted out in one long breathless sentence.

"Bravo!" said Paul, "If only the President of the United States, and all those other countries, had listened so well! Class is over for today. Now we have to take the Mercedes and get that canoe before some sea monster gets it. Just wait 'til you see the Mercedes; it will blow you away! Follow me kids."

That we did, through a game room with a pool table and ping-pong table, through a fully equipped machine shop and finally into a large garage. There sat the strangest vehicle I had ever seen. What had once been an expensive Mercedes sedan (I'd seen pictures of them) was now a wagon with a long tongue protruding out of the front. All of the front sheet metal and roof had been removed. There was no engine, no windshield, no front doors, and no trunk lid. The rear seat was removed as well, so that the rear area resembled the bed of a pickup truck. "So what do you think of that?" Paul asked.

Without really thinking before I spoke, I said, "Cool, how fast will it go?"

"That depends on what kind of mood our mules are in," he replied. At that very moment the garage door opened and in walked Mona leading two large mules by their bridles. Soon they were backed in on either side of the tongue and harnessed in place. For that they even let us help a little. I was thrilled; I had never been close to such large animals before. Snowball, on the other hand, looked anything but thrilled, but hopped up on Sara's lap as soon as she was in place in the middle of the front seat; Paul and I sat at the ends. "Fasten your seat belts!" said Paul; and off we went.

As soon as we started down the hill Paul began to use the break lightly to prevent the wagon from pushing the mules and he explained that the steering mechanism was attached to the tongue as a way of steering the mules, which was rarely required, since they knew the way most of the time. This time we were able to see the terrain we had trudged over the night before and it was an awesome panorama, both beautiful and sad.

On the way down, Paul explained that he was a "ham" radio operator and having hoarded a good supply of spare parts before hurricane Zandra, was able to keep in touch with other hams throughout the world. "In fact," he said, "I was talking to Hans in the Black Forest of Germany last evening. That is why my light was still on, my light that led you to find us. How lucky for us!"

Whispering in my ear, Sara said, "You know what Mom would say."

Continuing on, he told us about conditions in Germany and in many other parts of the world, how things like TV and computers were either limited or unusable now. The only business that seemed to be booming was small boat construction using local materials, mainly rowboats and sailboats.

That was Sara's cue to tell about our Aunt Kate rowing her boat all the way from Ohio. Paul said that she had to be the greatest champion rower of all time and he couldn't wait to meet her. "I know you are waiting to hear how we are going to get to New Orleans, and I am working on it," he said. "I am trying to reach a friend who owns a good sailboat, but he isn't answering my radio page. He is either out of power or not around. Try to be patient, kids. I know it's hard. Maybe someone else at the Crow's Nest can come up with a plan." With that he fell silent and remained so for the rest of the trip.

It was comforting to come gently to a stop and find the canoe just where we had left it. We unloaded the gear from the canoe and carried it up the steep embankment, stowing it behind the seat. Next came the canoe, which had to be tied down on the front end, since more than half stuck out of the rear. It was a truly ridiculous sight, but, with no one there to laugh at us, we laughed at ourselves. I recall that moment so vividly and the feeling of affection that came over me. It was a powerful feeling that Paul was my own father who had come back to life in order to care for us. It is a feeling that has never left me after all the intervening years.

That is when my sister fished out the waterproof packet that Mom had prepared containing the family photo, her memoir, and the letter to Uncle John. When Sara opened it and showed Paul the picture, it was clear that he was impressed. He studied the photo a long time, finally putting it back in Sara's hands and saying, "I can't wait to meet her. She is so beautiful, so much like you Sara. If I may, I would love to read her memoir. Do you suppose your mother would mind?"

Sara's response was immediate. "Of course not!" she said. "I'll keep it safe and you may borrow it any time."

"Good. As soon as time permits, I'll be knocking on your door. Thanks!" he said.

Before leaving, Paul pointed out a faded remnant of a Starbucks coffee house, close to where we were parked. "That was my favorite haunt once, back before hurricane Zandra. I used to roar down here in my fancy Mercedes and sip coffee and discuss politics with my friends. Well, the friends are mostly safe at the Crow's Nest, but the coffee is gone and I sure miss it. I've tried raising chicory as a substitute, but it doesn't come close to coffee. It's awful stuff!"

Then he showed us where they were taking apart buildings for reuse at the Crow's Nest, and some simply as firewood. Then he told us about the school on the farm where he hoped we might attend as long as we were there. There were about thirty students in all, ranging from preschool to college. He taught science and engineering to four of the college age. When we got back to the Crow's Nest we would meet them all and get the complete tour, he said. So with that to look forward to, we began the slow trip back up the hill.

As we rounded the last corner of the fence, Paul gave us a cheerful look and said, "Do you smell that? Tom 'the baker' is baking today so we all have fresh bread for supper. He does it once a week providing we can harvest enough grain for him. My, it smells good!" By this time in the afternoon our stomachs were really growling. Even "C" rations would have tasted good, but the prospect of fresh bread was divine.

We unloaded the canoe by the barn, and while there, we were shown the interior. Stored there were many hand tools and a few designed to be pulled by the mules. There was a tractor, obviously no longer used and a large strange shape under a dirty plastic cover. I ran over and peeked underneath; there sat a beautiful red airplane, it's wheels raised up to protect the tires. Paul looked amused by my excitement. "Another victim of the fuel shortage," he said. "I am going to be busy at my radio for awhile. Feel free to look around. Follow the road behind the barn and pay a visit to our village. Oh, and when you find the baker bring home our portion of bread for supper; just say that I sent you."

Up until now we had not seen anything that looked like a village, but as we walked along the path, Snowball trotting along behind, and rounded a copse of trees, there it was!

What a strange sight! It looked to my eyes like the pictures I had seen of Eskimo igloos, snow-white domes hugging the ground. There must have been at least fifty of them, all alike.

As we came closer a young woman came running from one of the houses to greet us. She had met us in the field that morning, she said; but we had met so many people, how could we be expected to remember all those names. "My name is Anne, spelled with an 'e'. There are several other women named Ann here, but I'm the only one with an 'e'. I specialize in making clothing since I was able to salvage my sewing machine. Biggest problem is finding cloth. But enough of my problems, do come and pay me a visit. And tell me about New Orleans. I declare, what a lovely city it was."

As Sara and I entered this unusual home we noticed that the walls were concrete and about 16 inches thick and painted white on the outside. Despite the heat of the sun outside, it was delightfully cool inside. The interior was one large open area except that a wooden structure comprising closets, a kitchen, a bathroom, and a second floor storage deck occupied the central area. One could tell that this was from lumber salvaged in the town we had come from. When I used the bathroom toilet I was not surprised to see that it was a composting version similar to the one in Paul's home.

There was a small fireplace that could also be used for cooking, but Anne said when it was sunny, she used only the small solar cooker outside. Then Anne showed us how the house collected rainwater. Just above the entrance door there was a trough that extended around the dome, sloping slightly to the rear. There it entered the house cistern just high enough to provide gravity feed to the kitchen and bath, and when the cistern was full the rainwater simply overflowed the outside trough.

This was one beautifully designed home! Even as a child I recognized the many advantages of this building, probably the most important being its strength in a serious storm. Anne confirmed that they had survived many of them. "It's all Paul's doin'," she said. "You all treat that man nice, hear? Why we never got to talk about New Orleans did we, and you gotta get a move on if you're gettin' bread. Why lookie here, here's my Bob comin' home for supper an all I'm doin' is gabbin'. Bob, you meet these nice kids and I'll get supper started."

Well, we made our meeting short and thanked them both. Then Bob showed us where the baker lived and, at a full run, we arrived breathless at his bakery. He met us at the door holding a basket with a long thin loaf of bread for us. This was Tom, the baker, and even though he appeared uncomfortably hot, he gave us a big grin and said, "Tell Paul my flour supply is holding pretty good for now. He'll be wanting to know, so remember to tell him now".

"We will, and thanks," said Sara, and we raced off with our treasure to find Paul. This time we just walked up to the big front door and walked right in, even though we felt uneasy doing that. The big house seemed so empty. We decided not to leave the bread in the kitchen for fear that Snowball might help herself. Then we heard the sound of someone talking and headed in that direction. We could hear a man talking in a foreign language, speaking very fast, and every so often Paul would respond in the same language. I assumed he was in radio contact with another country and since the door to this room was closed, we felt sure we shouldn't disturb him.

As we were going back to the kitchen, we heard the front door open and Mona joined us. "I'm here to fix supper and you kids can help," she said. Mona kept us busy all right, mostly peeling vegetables. While that was going on, she told us more about the farm operation. She explained that chickens and ducks, besides giving us delicious eggs to eat, were the only livestock raised for food. The goats gave us milk, reserved mostly for children, and spent much of their day eating the fast growing kudzu vines on the hillside. The goats were intelligent, adorable animals and they were NEVER to be eaten! Those were the only animals, besides the two mules, Paul would raise on the island, since you can feed more people per acre with vegetables and grain than is possible when raising livestock. When Sara asked if Paul minded our having Snowball, Mona said, "Of course not! Pets are family!"

The cooking was done this time on a small wood stove located on a wide flag-stoned veranda on the east side of the house. Mona told us that on most sunny days the solar stove was used, but it takes longer and today she just ran out of time. Out there on the veranda, shaded from the late afternoon sun, the heat from the stove was not unpleasant. There were potted flowers everywhere and sturdy furniture for sumptuous outdoor living. It was there that we set a table for supper while Mona went to get Paul.

Sara and I were in a festive mood, but Paul, when he sat down, was obviously depressed. Speaking more to Mona than to us, Paul related all the contacts he had made and what he had discovered. He had been able to reach several boat owners, people who had boats suited to the task of rescuing our mother and aunt. Recently, however, the government, in surprise visits, had confiscated their boats for "emergency governmental use" and compensated the owners with paper money (with little practical value). Any owner of a boat, in serviceable condition, twenty feet or more in length who did not comply would be prosecuted to the fullest extent of the law. "If it weren't so serious, it would be laughable!" said Paul bitterly. "Then I finally got through to the office of the National Coast Guard only to be told that they knew of no such practice (confiscating boats), and we would be put on their waiting list to receive help. Maybe in a couple months, they said. Mona, I wonder if I collected enough alcohol for the plane, I might fly up there and confront them eye-to-eye. What do you think?"

Sara and I kept very quiet while Mona pondered the question. Finally she shook her head and replied, "Paul, you know how some of them, especially the president, hate you for always being right. As it is, they have stopped giving you a hard time; raise trouble for them and they will make trouble for us. Don't risk it! Say, if Sara's Aunt Kate could row all the way from Ohio we can surely work something out! Now let's eat!"

That brightened the mood considerably. The food, although a bit strange to us, was delicious, especially the bread with goat butter and a glass of cold goat milk. We gave Paul the message from Tom about having sufficient grain for now and Paul replied, "Thank God for small blessings!"

"I did," said Sara.

It had been a big day and soon we were in bed and awaiting sleep.

JANUARY 14, 2049
THE KIDNAPPING

As we awoke on this day, we were greeted by the pounding of rain and the moaning of wind in the trees. Instinctively, we checked the ceiling for leaks and were delighted to find none. Racing to the kitchen, we were met by Paul holding a cup of steaming tea, and soon we were all sitting at the table eating a hearty breakfast with our host. Snowball, quite contented with Army "C" rations, ate on the floor.

Paul told us that we did need the rain both for the garden and to refill the cisterns. Besides, there was school on rainy days in the village and some of the older students would be walking in the door any minute. What an exciting idea it was to go to school with others of our age. Having been home-schooled by Mom we had craved the social interaction with other children, but I, at least, felt shy and intimidated by the prospect, as well.

When breakfast was over, Paul told us he had been thinking a lot about boat design. Then took us into his office to show us his ideas. There he had a large drawing board of the old-fashioned kind on which he had a layout drawing he wanted to show us. He was considering using two old propane gas tanks that were empty to make outriggers for the canoe in order to make it more stable, sort of a catamaran. It would require a motor of some kind, however, especially since we would be bucking the usual prevailing wind. "I might use the radial engine from my airplane to push it along, but what I really need is one of my friends with a good sailboat, someone beyond the reach of the US government," he grumbled, more to himself than to us.

Paul's office was a wonderful place for a boy. It was filled with toys (models and prototypes according to Paul) and as I remember back to the events that happened next, in such a bewildering blur, it barely seems real. I was playing with a model helicopter, making the "plop-plop-plop" sounds to myself when I became aware of the very same sound thundering just outside the building. Sara was tugging on my arm and shouting, "Run! NOW!" Paul was nowhere in sight and I began running after Sara now, half in a dream state of my imagination, half in a dawning state of sheer terror! I had no idea what was happening except that Sara was ahead of me and running fast. We were heading toward the garage where the Mercedes was parked, when a door opened just ahead of me and suddenly strong arms enveloped me and I was out in the rain. There it was! It was huge, black, and utterly terrifying, its giant rotor blades spinning. At the door of this monster more arms grabbed me. I could hear Sara screaming somewhere and I could hear Paul's voice, but now the roar of the engines increased to a fever pitch and I could feel the chopper rise into the air with a sickening, pulsing motion.

As I think back to that day, I suspect much more happened, but I was too bewildered. I could not hear Sara now and I could not see her. Had she escaped—or was she dead? I heard Paul talking very fast to someone in a language I could not follow, except for an occasional word that sounded like Spanish. I was tied now by a rope and had been pushed into a sitting position against the cold and vibrating hull of the helicopter. Someone was laughing now and I realized that we were the joke. We had been kidnapped!

I remember trying very hard not to throw up and the sense of victory when that feeling eased. My nose tickled, but my arms were tied down so that I couldn't scratch. Eventually that too eased. Once Paul tried to speak to me, to reassure me, I suppose, but someone struck him to make him stop. No one spoke after that, not even our captors. I was left with my troubled thoughts and the constant roar of the engine and the throb of the rotors.

I was crouched there, unable to move, and becoming very cold, when one of our captors wrapped a rough blanket over my shoulders and even tucked it behind my back. I asked him then to give Sara a blanket too. His reply, "Girl no come. Now you shut up mouth!" What a relief to hear those words! Sara was safe, and had not been kidnapped. With that reassurance and the warmth of the blanket and the numbing sound of the engine, I must have fallen asleep.

When I awoke the copter was on the ground, the door was open, sun streaming in, and best of all: Paul was standing above me smiling, a large bruise on his left cheek. I was helped to stand and the ropes were removed, whereupon Paul embraced me and whispered, "Call me 'Dad' and do what they say."

Paul helped me out of the copter, whereupon we were greeted by a well-dressed man, whom Paul seemed to know well. He was short in stature, heavy-set and almost completely bald. Paul introduced him as Dr. Emanuel Gucci from the University of La Paz, Bolivia. I was introduced as Paul's child.

My first impression was that this must be the man who had us kidnapped, and I was therefore puzzled by the way Paul interacted with him. He seemed friendly, but was he really our enemy? Something strange was going on. He acted as if he were the person in charge. Speaking to us as if we were his honored guests, he asked if we had been treated well, and Paul responded in the affirmative. I noticed that we still had military guards surrounding us and they looked anything but friendly, and they were leading us to a Lear jet that was parked nearby.

I was told to sit on the left side of the aircraft, Paul and Dr. Gucci on the other. Two guards sat behind the pilot facing us. The moment the door closed, the plane began to rumble down the runway rapidly picking up speed, pressing us firmly into our seat cushions. I must admit that my feelings at this point were somewhat confused: on the one hand riding in a Lear was a dream come true, on the other hand, we were being KIDNAPPED!

This part of the trip was pleasant enough, at least at the beginning. We were fed well and I was given comic books in Spanish. They were not funny, but it was a chance to brush up on the language. Paul and Dr. Gucci were in deep discussion apparently designing something, sketching and calculating. We were flying above the clouds so the view out the window soon grew tiresome.

I had plenty of time now to think about Sara and what might have happened to her. I remembered hearing her scream. I knew her screams well. It had been a scream of anger more than a scream of pain. I tried hard to convince myself of that. She was tough; she had escaped and was still at the Crow's Nest. She would find a way to save Mom.

We had been flying what seemed like many hours. It had been a long day and now as the plane began to approach the ground the sun was setting and the sharp contrasts between light and shadow gave a sense of drama to the landscape below. Now I could see a large city and more than half of it was under water. "This is Buenos Aires, Argentina, Will, at least what is left of it. As you see, they have flooding too," said Dr. Gucci. Paul was quietly studying the terrain below and made no comment.

Once the Lear had landed and come to a stop, the door was opened and a wave of moist warm air enveloped us. It was mid-summer here, which I knew, but the suddenness of the change still came as a surprise. We were quickly ushered outside and immediately moved to a limo. The front passenger seat of the limo was turned backwards with one of our somber faced guards still watching our every move.

Soon we were traveling up winding roads to a villa high in the hills overlooking the city.

It was beautiful here. Flowers bloomed in profusion and an extensive garden beckoned to us, but instead we were ushered into a side entrance of a large rambling building. Here the guard placed us in a small room, locking the door as he left. I was about to ask Paul a question, thinking we were alone at last, but a firm look from Paul made me change my mind; the room was probably bugged. Paul and Dr. Gucci made small talk with me, choosing their words carefully. We were "guests" in the governor's villa and we would have nothing to fear. We must do as we were bidden and I was not to ask too many questions. They, Dr. Gucci and Paul, were there to assist the Argentine scientists to solve a problem, he said. Paul nodded his head in agreement.

Soon we heard footsteps and the turning of a lock. Suddenly the door was opened wide and a small man in an ornate uniform stood before us; armed guards were close behind him. The man's chest was filled with colorful ribbons and he wore an outlandish red sash about his waist. My immediate impression of him was how much he resembled the pompous little rooster I had seen in the comic book aboard the plane!

Speaking in rather stilted English he said, "Let me introduce myself. I am Captain Francesco of Security. It is so good of you to have come to our rescue Dr. McMaster and Dr. Gucci. I regret any unpleasantness you may have felt at the beginning of your trip, but we intend to recompense you both well for your services. Our operatives do use much force at times, but I ask you, would you have accepted our invitation otherwise? Oh, and I see you have a young man with you. May I ask ..."

Here Paul cut him off with, "My son, William. You must treat him well if you wish my cooperation."

"Of course, Doctor." he replied. "Now if you will all follow me, I will show you to your suite where you can freshen up. Dinner will be served in about one hour. Your valet will provide you with suitable attire. You will dine with the Minister of Engineering tonight." With that we set off through a maze of hallways until we came to a beautiful four-bedroom suite complete with its own walled-in garden. It was beautiful with flowers and a fountain, but I noticed that the high garden wall was topped by razor wire, probably electrified.

As soon as the door was locked and we were alone, Paul hurried me to the garden where, in a whisper, he told me things that answered most of the questions that were nagging me. I must listen carefully and remember what he said. Argentina had become a ruthless dictatorship with a poor human rights record. Every move we made and everything we said in a normal voice was certainly being recorded. Dr. Gucci, his old friend and colleague, had also been kidnapped. He had been taken at gunpoint as he left the university where he taught. (I was relieved to know, for sure, that he was one of us.) Paul continued, saying that I must pretend to be his son, be polite, and be cautious when asked questions. He and Dr. Gucci had knowledge that these people needed desperately, so we would probably be treated well. If we were careful we would all get back home eventually. We must be very patient. Now we must take a shower and endure a formal dinner, dressed in fancy clothes, and answer a lot of questions.

While I was taking my shower, enjoying really warm water, the valet came to fit the men with tuxedos. The valet did not speak English. When he saw me he simply shook his head; he had nothing to fit a child. Then after much conversation and waving of arms, Paul and Dr. Gucci were led away to a formal dining room and I was fed a delicious supper in the garden, with a waiter watching over me—or maybe he was a guard in disguise. Believe me, this was such a relief to be served dinner this way. I felt like the boy in the <u>Prince And The Pauper</u>, a book by Mark Twain, that Mom had given me. I felt like the pauper child who, on a lark, changed places with the Prince of England. This was fun being served fine food, with a waiter standing by to do my bidding.

That got me thinking, however. Mom, poor Mom! Would I ever see Mom again? And how I wished Sara were here with me. Maybe Sara would save Mom's life and get all the glory, while I was here, being treated like a prince, which I certainly was not. Before I knew it the waiter was bending over me with genuine concern in his eyes, wondering why I was crying. It was a little hard to explain, but when I devoured everything on my plate he seemed less concerned.

Dinner over, I was left to my own devices. I sat in the garden, thinking of all the things that had happened to us, all in one day. The contrast between the start and the finish was staggering. Here I sat in this beautiful garden smelling the fragrance of the flowers, listening to the splash of water in the fountain, and studying the stars of the southern hemisphere. I had much to be thankful for: Paul and I were unhurt and would someday be sent home and Dr. Gucci was our friend, not our enemy. I began to think what Mom would say about all that, until sleep overtook me and I staggered into the bedroom to find the bed that was waiting for me.

JANUARY 14, 2049
SARA'S ACCOUNT

Will has asked me to write this next chapter recalling as best I can what happened on that awful day. Will was so wrapped up in his play, making believe, I suppose, that he was riding in a toy helicopter, that he never saw the masked gunmen take Paul from the office. I had to pull Will from the room. I think we both might have escaped if only he had run faster. When I saw what was happening I tried to join him, but the helicopter went up too fast and left me there screaming, on the ground. Even now, so many years later, I have nightmares about that huge whirling machine and Will disappearing inside it!

Then Mona came and put her arms around me and together we retreated to the house. The sound of the rain now seemed to be especially terrifying and it continued that way until evening. By this time almost all of the Crow's Nest inhabitants were gathered at the house and almost as many theories had been expressed about what had occurred, none of them very comforting.

Mona, it appeared, was now in charge. She wanted to know every detail of what I had seen that morning, markings on the chopper that might identify the country of origin, the language of their voices, anything! I was not much help. After that she spent much time on the radio searching for answers. Her first call was to the CIA, since the kidnapping of a US citizen, especially a scientist of Dr. McMaster's stature, was cause for action by the US government. The CIA was interested all right! Mona spent much of the day on the radio with first one office and then another. Finally, they assigned a special agent to handle the case and a special access code to reach him if any new information should surface. They asked me a lot of questions too. They were already following up on leads, they said, and might come to interview me in person. Mona had her own list of suspects, Argentina being one of them, but by late evening she had no confirmation of anything. She felt pretty sure the kidnappers were not seeking ransom, but rather the particular skills and knowledge that Paul possessed. Mona was obviously correct in this assumption.

Mona moved her things to the McMaster's house that night, after the rain stopped. This way she could monitor the radio and better watch over me. That night we moved two cots into Paul's office and slept side-by-side, one ear listening for the crackle of the radio. None came. Snowball jumped up beside me and stayed there all through the night. She seemed to sense that I was scared and troubled. I wondered where Will was, and if he was safe? Her purring did make me feel better, and allowed me to get some sleep.

JANUARY 15, 2049
ARGENTINA

It was very dark when I awoke from a terrifying dream. Wide awake now, the dream still haunting me, I felt a presence in the room that made me almost afraid to breathe. Someone was there. Having just awakened, my pupils were open wide, but despite this I could see no one in the dim light. Feeling a bit foolish now, and needing to relieve myself, I got out of bed and headed toward the bathroom.

Suddenly from behind me an arm clamped me about the middle and a hand, smelling of tobacco, was covering my mouth! Helpless now, I was lifted off the floor and carried out to the center of the garden. There, clearly visible in the starlight (there was no moon) stood Paul with Dr. Gucci beside him, both motioning with their finger to their lips to be quiet. Released now from my captor I was hugged by Paul. Whispering in my ear, Paul introduced me to the man who had grabbed me, a large dark-haired fellow, maybe thirty years old, named Pedro. Paul said he was helping us escape and that he would explain more later.

When I told Paul about my need to use the bathroom, he surprised me. He said to go and make all the usual noises, then climb back in bed, blow my nose hard—and then very quietly come back to join them. I did exactly as told and soon we were following Pedro into a garden tool room, for which Pedro had a key. We walked carefully to a door at the far end, which opened onto a large walled-in courtyard. Here I could make out tractors, trucks and carts: the equipment to operate the farm that supplied the villa. Here too, the wall was topped with razor wire.

Just as Pedro was unlocking the large entrance gate in the wall, we heard the loud whinny of a horse, apparently from a stable in the courtyard. We froze. We were about to step through the open gate, when suddenly floodlights came on, bathing us in light. It was over! We had been discovered!

We were running now between rows of fruit trees. Somewhere behind us a motorcycle engine roared into life, then another. We were on a dirt road now and when Pedro leapt into the ditch and crawled into a cement culvert, we all followed. Paul crawled in last and placed a trembling hand protectively on my shoulder. Never had I felt such a rush of emotion as I felt lying there in the muddy water feeling Paul's loving touch. I felt at that moment that my father had truly returned to me in the form of Paul. I remember wanting to tell him so, but I could not.

When first one, then another motorcycle roared over our culvert, Pedro crawled to the far end to emerge into rough wooded terrain. Here in the shelter of trees, we stopped for a moment to catch our breath and as Dr. Gucci and Pedro conferred about the best plan of escape, I was hoisted to Paul's back. We traveled several hours in this manner, except that soon, at my insistence, I was walking on my own again.

The sky was beginning to brighten when we emerged from the woods into cleared farmland. There, tucked among the trees, was a small barrio of about six houses, huts really. As we approached the first hut a dog began to bark furiously and soon a man dressed in a nightshirt peered through a window, then slowly opened the door.

This time it was Pedro who did the talking. He must have said all the right things because we were soon sitting at their table, sipping coffee (real coffee) and eating fried bread resembling pancakes with honey. The man's wife was graciously inviting me to eat my fill, but Paul gave me a look that told me not to be piggy! The dog was introduced to us as Noche, (night) because of his jet-black hair. I was pleased to see that he was now wagging his tail. The men were all conferring, exchanging money and shaking hands; they would help us.

We would travel by day to avoid suspicion. They had a crop of potatoes ready to be taken to the market that was, fortunately, close to the docks. We could be safely hidden in the back of his donkey cart under partially filled sacks of potatoes to avoid detection from copters and police. At the market the farmer had friends who would love the opportunity to confound the police by getting us passage on a ship, probably a merchant ship. Finding a ship going where we wished to go—well, that was a different matter.

Shaking hands on the plan, we went to the barn and helped the farmer harness the donkey and load a layer of straw, followed by potato sacks in the bottom of the cart. Next we prepared a number of partly filled sacks, laid down as comfortably as possible on the bumpy load and let the farmer cover us up with more potatoes. Then the farmer's wife came out to give her opinion and after making many adjustments to our disguise, sent us off down the long road to market. Noche sat proudly on the seat beside his master.

Well, I have had a few very trying experiences in my life, but none that I recall came close to this trip. The three men, all of them large, filled the bed of the wagon, leaving just enough room for me to fit crosswise by their heads. This brought my head next to Pedro's, which allowed us to talk quietly to each other. He told me about the adventures he had as a child in their mountain village in Bolivia, tending his father's sheep. He had a brother that was two years older than he, so we compared notes on having a bossy sibling to deal with. I, of course, told the tale of my life in our drowned city. He agreed that he'd had it better in the mountains. When he told me about sledding down the mountains, as a boy, in dazzling white snow, and how bitter cold it was, it made me extremely envious. Somehow, it seemed to make the steamy heat of the sun, which was roasting us, feel even worse. Pedro had a different opinion. He said, "Really think HARD about that snow and it will cool you down."

I had a thin piece of cloth over my eyes and nose to keep dust out, but it got to me anyway. With my eyes open I could see a little through the cloth and between the pota-

toes. I got air, but with the bouncing of the cart on the rut-
ted dirt road, the dust was terrible. Once I got to sneezing
so bad, the farmer had to stop and cover me up again.
Lucky for us, no one was watching.

It must have been noon when the cart came to a stop
under a grove of trees next to a swift flowing river. Here we
got out from under the sacks to eat the meal that the
farmer's wife had prepared for us. There was not a soul
there. What a relief it was to rest and move about. It was
safe here, we were told; the water was clean so we could
even swim. Noche had plunged into the water the moment
we arrived, but Paul shook his head when I showed an
interest in doing the same.

At the rivers edge floated a raft with a rope attached that
extended to the far shore, over a pulley at a tree, then back
to a crude capstan on the ferry where it was wrapped
around twice, then to a tree on our side and then to the raft
again, forming a loop. Paul explained to me that this was a
simple do-it-yourself ferry. As soon as we had eaten we got
the cart and donkey onto the raft, holding back on the
wheels as it rolled down the steep bank. Finally, all in place
we were ready to cross.

Crossing in this way was slow work and the danger of
being spotted from the air was great, so we covered ourselves under the potatoes again. Pedro remained with the
farmer, however, to help turn one of the capstan cranks. He
would hide under the cart if an aircraft showed up. Happily
none did and the crossing was made without a problem.

When we reached the other side, the farmer cheerily told
us that we had "only" about thirty kilometers to go. This

was not cheering news, but because the road soon became smoother and I had arranged my potato bed a bit better, I actually went sound asleep and had to be awakened because I was snoring! Now I could hear people, lots of people. I could hear the farmer greeting friends, shouts and laughter. Finally the cart stopped and the farmer said he would be right back, but would leave Noche to guard the cart. Speaking broken English, he said he had to make "arrangements," and for us to stay very, very still because police were everywhere. This, of course, made it almost impossible to lie still! I itched all over.

It is difficult to measure time under circumstances such as this, but I am sure the "arrangements" took over an hour. It was growing dark when the farmer returned with another man and the two, standing close to the cart, discussed our escape. They spoke Spanish so I understood little of what they said, but it was clear from their speech that they were both quite drunk. Finally, the cart, with the farmer, his friend, and Noche all crowded on the front seat, began to move slowly through a series of dark streets. Now I heard a rumble that proved to be a large sliding door closing behind us, and the slurred command of the farmer to "get out fast." This we did! What a relief to stand again and brush the dust from our clothes.

The building proved to be a large unlighted warehouse, empty except for us. Now the farmer's friend introduced himself, and in Spanish, talked at length with the men. (Paul in turn translated for my benefit.) Money was the chief topic. He was running great risk in helping us and the guards at the dock demanded large bribes to look the other way. Pedro was, fortunately, prepared for this, since bribery was a way of life in Argentina. In the end, the man seemed satisfied, so the negotiations continued.

The only ship that was ready to sail was a merchant bound for Italy. It would sail in about an hour. To wait for a ship to the US would be suicidal. He knew the captain, who, of course, would need to be well recompensed. Pedro said it would happen. The men shook hands and bidding the farmer and Noche, "goodbye," we were ushered into a small office where the man drew the blinds before switching on a light.

Now for the first time I could see the man clearly. He had a very red face and was heavy set wearing an ornate uniform that was about a size too small. The desk displayed a sign that identified him as Captain Contonio, Commissioner of Shipping. We were invited to use his rest room and make ourselves comfortable. When I returned from the rest room he was talking rapidly on the telephone waving his free arm excitedly as he spoke. At this point a thought crossed my mind: had we had fallen into a trap? The calm expression on Paul's face, however, set my mind at ease. This man cared only for our bribe money; the law meant nothing!

He stood up now behind his desk and said, "It is time. We must move quickly. The ship is about to sail." This time we were hustled into the back of a large van; there were no seats or windows. With Captain Contonio at the wheel, we stopped at the guard station. After a few murmured remarks to the guards, the gate opened and we passed through. Now traveling at high speed we passed by several empty wharfs to a large and very rusty container ship and screeched to a halt just as a tractor was about to pull away the gangplank. After much horn blowing and waving of arms (and curses I could not understand), we were all allowed on board leaving a beaming Commissioner of Shipping standing on the wharf below us. We had made it by the skin of our teeth!

The moment we were on board we were led to a small lounge next to the bridge and told to wait there until the captain was free to talk to us. I wanted to go on deck to watch the ship maneuver away from the dock, but Paul shook his head. He explained that there would be plenty of time for that after we were at sea, so I stood by a window that separated us from the bridge and imagined that it was I, Captain William Anchor, who was master of the ship!

Just then the real master stepped into the room and introduced himself as Captain Andersen of the Swedish container ship, Norse Princess. He had a bushy white beard and a wide smile, in my mind a real Santa Claus look-alike. After shaking hands and talking at length with Pedro, Paul and Dr. Gucci, he came to me and said, (speaking perfect English now), "I'll bet you would like to see how this ship works. I'm sure your father will let me give you a tour of the bridge before you go to bed. Tomorrow, when I am free, you can go with me when I inspect the ship. Is that alright Dr. McMaster?"

The answer, of course, was a "yes" and thus began the most delightful adventure of my entire life. That night, after a supper I barely tasted, I was shown to a bunk with high sides, right above Paul's, in a neat cabin for just the two of us. It had been a really long day so I was asleep the moment my head touched the pillow.

JANUARY 15, 2049
SARA'S ACCOUNT

I must have been crying in my sleep because Snowball was licking my face. She was such an understanding cat. She seemed to feel my grief at losing Will. What would I tell Mom when I saw her,—if I ever saw her? My whole world had been ripped apart. I was having a pretty good cry and feeling quite sorry for myself, when in walked Mona and gave the thumbs-up. She had good news, she said.

While I was sleeping she had received word that a Coast Guard rescue launch was finally being dispatched to help Mom. It would stop to pick me up at the beach at 10:00 AM tomorrow so that I could direct them to our house. Apparently the priorities had changed since the kidnapping of one of the nation's top scientists. Previously snubbed, now Dr. McMaster was embraced as the brilliant environmentalist that he was. Now the "red carpet" was being rolled out for him and anyone associated with him. Things were looking up!

I cannot recall what else went on that day except the search I made to find a suitable gift to give Mom when I saw her. I finally settled on a bouquet of flowers, which I would pick in the morning so they would be fresh. That decided, I was eventually able, with Snowball's help, to sleep that night. The night before, sadness hampered my sleep; this night it was happiness!

JANUARY 16, 2049
THE NORSE PRINCESS

The day began with Paul shaking me awake. I was to shower, using a special soap for salt water (fresh water was reserved for drinking) and hurry to breakfast with the captain. My filthy clothes had been washed during the night and were waiting on a chair beside me. You can bet I moved fast! When I entered the mess, right on time, Captain Andersen motioned for me to sit beside him. Paul, Dr. Gucci and Pedro sat across from us. The conversation soon turned to technical matters involving the changes that had occurred in the Earth and how best to cope with them. I, of course, added little to the conversation, but felt privileged to listen in. That is what I wanted to be some day, a scientist and maybe a sea captain too!

Now turning to me, the captain asked if I had slept well. Captain Andersen (I was always to address him that way) said he had a grandson in Sweden who was just my age and how he was sure to become a captain himself some day. Perhaps he would be in charge of one of the new wind-solar hybrids that had only recently been commissioned. These ships were wonderful since they produced no carbon dioxide to worsen global warming.

When breakfast was over, he led me back to the bridge. He showed me everything on the bridge again and asked me questions to see what I remembered from the evening before. I guess my answers pleased him because now he took me on a tour of the entire ship. When we entered the engine room he gave me earmuffs to protect my hearing. The sight and sound of the huge machinery that turned the screws was simply breathtaking! There was a junior officer with us and sometimes the captain gave him an order to carry out. I asked many questions, silly ones I'm sure, but he never made me feel put down and gave me detailed answers. He explained the ship's rules that I too must obey, and introduced me to many of the crew. He made me feel as if I belonged!

We returned to the bridge on the open deck walking beside the huge containers, stacked three high. From there, the ocean looked endless and sparkling clean; a region of purity the like of which I had never seen before. The sea air filled my lungs and tugged at my hair. I wanted to stay on deck, but the captain said I was already getting red and it would be better to get a good tan in short periods, since a person sunburns faster on the sea. He promised me that as long as I followed the rules, I could have the run of the ship during our voyage; the engine room, however, was off limits.

When I asked him to tell me about rogue waves, huge waves I had heard of that can sometimes sink a ship, the captain grew very serious. Yes, he had seen them. These freak waves travel very fast and are very dangerous. The trick, as he explained it, is to turn into the wave, if you have had sufficient warning about the direction it is traveling. Next, the ship must have sufficient momentum to plunge through without being twisted sideways. "If we survive all that, lad, you will have a great story to tell your grandchildren," he said, smiling broadly. "If you ask your father about how they are caused, he can explain it better than I. Now don't look so worried, lad, rogue waves are very rare," he said, his hand patting my shoulder.

By this time we had arrived back at the bridge and the captain told me that, since he had work to do, I should leave him now and join the men in the lounge. When I walked in I found them all deeply involved in discussion. The table was littered with papers, some with sketches, some with calculations. I stood and watched for a while, then took a seat and continued to study these men at work. They were all too involved to take note of my presence. This was how engineers and scientists worked. It was a realm of ideas and numbers; it was all over my head, but I was fascinated. (Now, as an old man, I seem to remember that scene as the time I became certain that I too would follow a similar path, as indeed I did, but in the field of botany and agriculture.)

I really wanted to be outside, however, so I went out onto a small platform at the port end of the bridge. The ship was moving northeast so I was shaded from the brilliant morning sun. From this vantage point I could see the entire length of the port side from prow to stern. Large dark gulls, "gooney birds" I was told later, flew low behind the ship until they overtook it, then swinging away, circled to a position far behind, and repeated the pattern. They were searching for food scraps from the ship. I looked for whales and porpoises too, but none were visible. It was fun to watch the hypnotic wash of the bow wave, pure white with tinges of emerald green. And flying fish, if that is what they were, seemed to skip from wave top to wave top, always where I was not looking, right at the edge of my field of vision. It was tantalizing.

This glorious scene occupied my thoughts for some time, but then I began to think back to all the incredible things that happened to me in such a short time, and what Sara might be doing, and Mom. Would I ever see any of them again? I even began to feel a sense of shame for feeling so happy with the wind in my face and the expanse of the ocean all about me. They seemed so far away; they WERE far away. (I had a pretty good sense of geography, from Mom's teaching). How was it possible for me to be so far from home? And going toward Italy wasn't getting us much closer!

Suddenly, I felt a warm hand rest on my shoulder and looked up to see Paul looking down at me. All he said was, "Beautiful isn't it." and leaned on the handrail beside me. He seemed to know just what I had been thinking because he soon was explaining things that had puzzled me. Was he able to use the ship's radio to contact Mona and Sara? No, since the Argentines would pick up the transmission and likely come after us. We must be patient and wait until we reached Europe, which would take about two weeks. Who was Pedro? Pedro was a former graduate student of Dr. Gucci's who had unfortunately taken a job offer in Argentina before it became a ruthless dictatorship. Under the current government, he would not have been allowed to just quit, so when he recognized Dr. Gucci, he decided to risk his life and help us all escape. That was extremely brave of him. If caught by the Argentines, he would surely be executed for defecting. And what was Italy going to be like? Italy would be both very beautiful and very friendly. Paul said he had a number of close friends there and our stay should be very pleasant. Then he said jokingly, "You may like it so much, you won't want to leave!" Finally, he said the words I most wanted to hear, "We'll get home, Will, and when we do, what a story you will have to tell, my boy!"

That afternoon a squall blew up and rain pelted the windows of the captain's lounge. I had come inside, of course, and was now exploring the books that lined the walls. There I came across <u>Two Years Before The Mast</u> by Dana, the true story of a trip around Cape Horn, the southern tip of South America, on a windjammer, long before the invention of the steamship. This was the perfect book for stormy days at sea. Since the bridge area was high above the water, the motion of the ship was considerable, so, with book in hand, I staggered to a comfortable chair, falling in, rather than sitting down. I was comforted to see that the chair was bolted to the floor and that, apparently, none of the others saw me fall into it. Maybe I was not quite ready to be a seaman yet!

JANUARY 16, 2049
SARA'S ACCOUNT

I am an early riser by nature, but this morning I beat all previous records. I picked the flowers that I planned to give Mom, while the daylight was so faint I could barely distinguish their colors. Yesterday, the baker had provided me with a loaf of his delicious bread and a container of goat butter to go with it. I was ready. Mona had breakfast cooking. I told her I wasn't hungry, but she said, "Eat anyway. Don't make me have to stuff it down your throat!" Soon we were both laughing so hard that neither of us could eat. We were both giddy with happiness.

We were to be at our beach, (mud flat is more like it), by 10AM, but wisely planned to be there much earlier, just in case. The carpenter was coming down with us so that he and Mona could retrieve a load of used lumber to take back. Mona would return to the Crow's Nest after I was safely on the Coast Guard boat.

It was 8AM by my watch when we climbed aboard the Mercedes. Even the mules seemed to catch the happy mood and moved with uncharacteristic speed. On the way down, Mona gave me the Crow's Nest radio call letters so that I might contact her by radio from the boat. We assumed that Mom would go to a hospital somewhere and that I would go with her. Mona stressed that she and I must never lose touch and we hugged on that.

Well, to make a long story short, 10 AM came and went, but no Coast Guard appeared. The same for 11,12,1,2,3 and 4PM. All three of us worked collecting lumber to fill the back of the Mercedes. Then we unhitched the mules and let them graze. Mona, bless her, had the foresight to bring food, just in case, so we too ate. The waiting, however, was just intolerable!

Then at 4:11 PM, by my watch, we heard the sound of an engine and then picked out the boat, a mere speck on the horizon. Mona told me she had warned them about the sunken train, the one that we had almost struck with the canoe, but there was a lot more junk out there to avoid. We, of course, were suddenly energized and waved a white cloth on the end of a board to be sure they saw us. They did! When they were about a hundred yards out they lowered a yellow inflatable dingy and rowed up to meet us.

What a moment that was! They were so nice. They apologized for being late. They had gotten a distress call from a capsized boat, and emergencies come first. They thanked Mona for the GPS coordinates and said we were "right on". On board now with my flowers, my bread and butter and my map of New Orleans, Mona and the carpenter pushed us off.

When I climbed aboard the Coast Guard boat I was treated like a celebrity. We would travel in relatively safe shallow water for most of the trip, they said, going east of New Orleans out into the Gulf of Mexico, and approach the city from there. We would arrive in the morning. I showed them the map and pointed out the location of our house. The boat had a shallow draft, they said, and was narrow enough to travel the streets all the way to Mom's front door, if it was deep enough, but if we had a tight space we could always use the dingy. "Piece-a-cake," they said.

Next I talked to the doctor and told him all I knew about Mom's condition, which wasn't much. He told me that they were giving Mom the deluxe treatment, having him on board, because usually they only had EMTs who received advice from a doctor by radio. I was impressed by his statement; somehow the Anchor family had "come up in the world", a clear consequence of our association with Paul, Dr. Paul McMaster. There was a bit of politics involved here!

I was ushered into the mess after that. The galley was next to it and the aroma of fine food was tantalizing. To my surprise, I was introduced to a TV reporter and asked to take a seat opposite him at the table. Just relax and be myself, he said, and yes, I would be on the evening news! I was told to just ignore the camera and answer his questions. As I look back at that event, it all happened so fast I had no time to get all flustered. I had so much to say, all bottled up inside me, that I just let it pour out. I gave that man the scoop of a lifetime! I must have talked for an hour, and when I finally saw myself on TV, some time later, it had been trimmed to about two minutes, and the message was somehow different from what I intended. (More politics at work!)

After supper, which was delicious, I went on deck to enjoy the fresh air and watch the sun set. It was glorious! We were already out of sight of land and it seemed strange to think that this had all been dry land a few decades earlier. I had been told to keep my life jacket on at all times. When I told a Coast Guardsman beside me at the rail that I thought we were going very fast, he laughed and said we were really going very slow because there might be flotsam floating in the water. "You'd really have to hang on tight if we were going fast!" he said.

The boat I was on was called a Search and Rescue Craft and the crew was very small. They worked in two shifts, day and night, with only enough bunks for one crew. That night I was shown to a bunk, recently occupied by a sailor, but made up with fresh linen for me. For privacy I had a curtain. The head was "unisex", but had a sound latch on the door. Back in the bunk I felt nurtured and safe. AND, WE WOULD SEE MOM IN THE MORNLNG! The roar of the engines soon put me to sleep.

JANUARY 17, 2049
THE NORSE PRINCESS

I awoke this morning to the sound of pounding rain. It came in sudden shuddering gusts making the entire ship tremble with its force. Paul, who was already dressed, came over and leaned against my bunk. "Aren't you glad you're not canoeing in this?" he said with a smile. It was a question not requiring an answer. I just smiled back.

I got up and dressed myself. I found, to my relief, that I was better at keeping my balance than I had been the evening before. I was getting my "sea legs". Down in the mess, a little later, I had another pleasant surprise: food looked more inviting than it had the evening before. I wasn't a "landlubber" any longer!

Back at the captain's lounge, I was about to settle in with my book, when Paul motioned me over to a table holding several books and paper. It was a school day, he said, and shoved a pad of paper in front of me. "Let's see how much your mother taught you," he said. "I'll test you on a few things so I know how much you know and where your talents lie. Then we will go on from there. OK?"

It certainly was "OK"; it was just what I wanted. I wanted to show what I was "made of" and I was eager to learn more. I had dozens of questions; now maybe I would get the answers. To begin with, he gave me a series of problems involving simple math, each subsequent one a bit more challenging. Some of them stumped me; others did not. After about four hours in this vein we stopped for a break. Paul leaned back in his chair and said, "Will, I can't wait to meet your mother. She is one top-of-the-line teacher; and you, Will, you are one smart kid. Lets see if I can teach you even more so you can surprise your mother when we meet her. Now, let's have lunch. School's over for the day. Tomorrow, tell me about what you have read in Two Years Before The Mast. I've read it; it's a wonderful tale and it's true. That is your homework assignment," he said. Lunch tasted fabulous after that.

Thus began a pattern of work mixed with pleasure that extended throughout the trip to Italy. Paul and I had school together each morning; afternoons were mine to roam the ship, read or visit with my new friends. It was a fine two weeks, fifteen days actually. I got to know Pedro well during our time together. He liked to play chess and taught me a number of clever moves, but we were not evenly matched, so he always won. Cards were better; there I had an equal chance and sometimes "beat the pants off of him!" He taught me Spanish and Portuguese while I taught him "American" English. Dr. Gucci, on the other hand, was harder for me to get to know. He was always polite, but kept me at a distance..

JANUARY 17, 2049
SARA'S ACCOUNT

When I got up next morning we were moving slowly northward toward the city I called home. It filled the skyline in the ghostly morning light. When I stepped on deck I saw the same sailor who had spoken to me the evening before and leaned on the rail beside him. The water here was filled with flotsam that bumped and scraped against the hull. "That's mostly garbage from the Mississippi," he said, "No need to worry though 'cause this baby is jet propelled and got no prop to snag nothin', understand? By the way, you sleep OK?"

I told him, "Sure," which wasn't quite true. I had slept at first, but then an awful dream had shocked me awake. In my dream, Mom was not at home, and I raced from room to room in the old house, but could not find her! I kept telling myself that this was only a dream and I was getting like Will, who believed in ghosts and dreams, and all such nonsense. I, Sara Anchor, had my head on straight! It didn't work, unfortunately, so I just lay there and pretended to sleep.

About then I was invited in for breakfast. It was good, but I barely tasted it. During breakfast I was surrounded by the men who would be rescuing Mom, all asking questions about water level at the house, shape of the porch, location of the door, etc. The weather was perfect, they said, and I was not to worry about a thing.

When I came back on deck, I found that our boat had crept in very close to the waterfront and the crew was preparing the inflatable dingy. I was told that the dingy would go into the city first, checking depths and for other obstacles that might prevent the boat from going all the way to my house. The doctor and I were to ride with them to the house!

The dingy used a small outboard motor this time and I was placed in back, map in hand, beside the sailor who held the tiller. It was a thrill to be navigator, but even more, to be going home! Another sailor and the doctor rode up front to watch for obstructions. Soon we were purring down watery streets, stopping often to measure the water's depth (with a simple pole), and several times reversing direction to find a better route. Finally we were on my street and my house was there just as I had left it about ten days before! I felt like calling out to hail our arrival, but no sound came out of my mouth. There was Kate's rowboat, resting on the porch. I could barely contain myself when the dingy gently scuffed up beside it, and I leapt onto the porch and raced to the front door.

The door was locked. This was strange; we never locked it. I pounded on the door, then ran and peered in a window. Everything looked normal. I decided they must be asleep so I pounded harder. After a minute, I was handed a bullhorn and shown how to use it. My voice came through it terribly loud, "Mom, Aunt Kate, I'm back!" After the echo and reecho, all I heard was the sound of my own breathing and the cry of gulls.

"Do you mind if I break open a window, Miss Anchor?" someone said. They were so polite. Of course I gave permission and a moment later the door flew open and I was racing up the stairs shouting my arrival. The bedroom was empty. Mom's bed and Kate's cot were side by side; both were unmade. I continued to race through the old house checking the bathroom, the third floor room we called the gym, the attic—nothing! It just couldn't be! It was my nightmare all over again. They were gone!

The Coast Guardsmen were more thorough and much calmer in their search. After I had been to every room and closet for a second time, even the house next door where we used the abandoned stove, and the roof garden, I had returned to Mom's room and crumpled onto her bed in a torrent of tears. I had lost Will and now I'd lost Mom! I was lying there sobbing, when I felt a gentle hand on my shoulder and a voice said, "I think we have something here, Miss, would you look at this?" It was the doctor. "We found it on the hood above the kitchen range. Looks like someone else came to save them first." It was a note in Kate's bold style (all caps) that said:

HAVE RIDE TO HOSPITAL AND MUST GET SISTER HELP FAST. NOT SURE WHERE WE ARE GOING. WILL SEARCH FOR SARA AND WILLIAM ANCHOR IN LOST CHILDREN DATABASES. BEST I CAN DO.

KATE 1/9/2049

I must have read that note a dozen times before the full import really sank in. Mom was already at a hospital, and that was good news, but I had no idea where, and that was bad. All in all, I now felt a lot better. The doctor gave me a handkerchief and I used it so thoroughly that he suggested I keep it. We had to go, he said, we had no time to linger. I hastily grabbed several of Mom's framed pictures and followed him down the stairs and out to the dingy. As we pulled away I took one last look at the house I knew as home. I have never seen it since.

The trip back to the Crow's Nest was uneventful. Mona had been contacted by radio and was on the beach to meet me. Everyone was so very kind to me, sensing my disappointment and helping me see the bright side. Soon I did, too. How hard could it be to contact all the hospitals by radio and find Mom?

Snowball was there to meet me too; and that night, she joined me in bed and made me feel truly at home.

FEBRUARY 2, 2049
NAPLES, ITALY

It was the second of February when our ship slowed to a stop at the port of Naples in Italy. By this time the thrill of the open sea had worn pretty thin and the thrill of seeing land had replaced it. Oh how beautiful those Italian mountains looked in the evening sun. Paul stood beside me on deck explaining the things that were going on: the tug boat that would ease us into the dock, the massive crane that would lift the containers and place them gently onto railroad cars or trucks, the electronic inspection of the containers for dangerous cargo without having to open the doors, and so much more. Italy, he said, had dealt with the lowering land mass problem better than many of the other nations and we would be treated extremely well here, since he had many friends and was well respected for his work.

Paul said that the evening before, while I was asleep, he had reached Mona by radio. Now they knew we were alive and well and where we had been. Mona, in turn, told him that Will's mom was at a hospital somewhere. He told me about Sara's adventure with the Coast Guard and hastened to add that we would surely be able to find Mom soon. How many hospitals can there be? Piece of cake!

I found it fascinating to watch the harbor craft and the longshoremen at work. Soon a gangplank was rolled into place and we were allowed to disembark. Captain Andersen was by our side inviting us, all four of us, to an evening meal at an exclusive club to which he belonged. There were taxis, strange vehicles, like rickshaws pulled by a smoky motorcycle, but we walked. I heard Paul mutter, "I thought those things had been banned."

The walk turned out to be mostly a climb, up staircase after staircase, eventually reaching the restaurant, perched right on the edge of the cliff we had climbed. When we reached the entrance, the maitre d' addressed Captain Andersen by name and led us to a table on the deck overlooking the harbor. It was spectacular! The ship below us looked so small from there. I had run to the railing to look down, but I heard Paul clear his throat and knew I must come to the table and behave myself. After all, I was eleven years old and should act my age. Before I could move, however, Captain Andersen was beside me, pointing out and naming the many sights. When Paul cleared his throat the second time, we both had to hurry to the table; the waiter was waiting.

Well, I won't go into details about the meal, except to say that it was delicious and there was far too much food. It was dark when we finished and the candles on the table had been lighted. I was allowed to stand by the rail enjoying the view while the men debated global environments and politics. The scene below me was one that I wanted to memorize in detail so that I could describe it to Sara and Mom. The city lights, I'd never seen so many lights in one place, twinkling like stars, and the haunting dark backdrop of the mountains, remains with me these many years later.

We said farewell to Captain Andersen that evening and thanked him for his hospitality. He took me aside then and gave me a remembrance of our friendship. It was a Dutch coin, a guilder. The Netherlands, he said, had basically been washed from the face of the earth by the rising waters, like the fabled city of Atlantis. As elsewhere, most of the people survived, but they had to move great distances to higher ground. The guilder was a coin of a lost land, he said. I thanked him profusely and have kept it in my pocket as a "good luck charm" ever since.

The next few days were a blur of activity. Paul and Dr. Gucci were in a seemingly continuous discussion with some "high level" people in the Italian government, while Pedro and I traveled about Naples and enjoyed the sights. It was winter there and the air was fresh and cool, especially in the mountains. Pedro knew enough Italian to get by and I picked it up as fast as possible. Together we had a great time without spending much of the precious money that Pedro kept in a well-hidden pouch, tucked in his armpit! Pedro joked that no one would steal his money if they knew it had been kept there!

Finally, one evening at our hotel, Paul advised us all that the US was sending a plane to take us to New Washington (the new Washington, partially rebuilt high on the Appalachian Mountain Range about 100 miles west of the old, flooded Washington DC). We should be ready to leave the hotel at 4AM the next morning, 2/7/2049. A chopper would take us to the Rome airport. A top-level meeting was scheduled for us all with the president as soon as we arrived in Washington and had been "debriefed." Wow! Suddenly we were very important people!

I thought Paul's reaction to this was a bit strange. He did not seem excited by it at all; amused would be a better word. "Maybe the 'prez' is coming around at last," he said with a grin. "Don't get your hopes up too high, though, and 'keep yer powder dry' in case he is ready to listen." Then, to me he said, "Be very polite when you meet him and always call him Mr. President or sir. Got it?"

"Yes, sir," said I.

FEBRUARY 7, 2049
ROME

If I slept at all that night, it couldn't have been much. By this time I had a complete set of new clothes, in fact, we all, long ago, discarded the things we had worn in the donkey cart. We were to meet the president so Paul had me properly dressed for the interview. When we went to get the chopper the elevator went UP and there on the roof of our hotel it stood waiting. This time the ride was a delight. Looking down on the lovely Italian landscape in the early morning light and mentally comparing this trip to the hellish one I had endured a month before; what a difference!

In Rome, which I saw little of, we landed on a vast area of tarmac and were escorted to a huge aircraft with <u>Air Force One</u> lettered on the side. There were two soldiers by the entrance; no bad people were going to get on that plane. As soon as we had climbed the steps and entered, the stair was raised and the door locked. We were shown to a sort of lounge and as soon as the seat belts were fastened I felt the plane begin to roll to our runway for takeoff. Was I very excited about it? Well, not really, I told myself; I was a pretty seasoned traveler by now!

After the plane had leveled off above the clouds, a man in a dark suit entered the lounge and began briefing the men about the upcoming meeting with the president. He sat with his back to me and spoke so softly that I could barely hear, and perhaps I was not intended to hear. I gathered that we had embarrassed the CIA. Apparently they had sent a SWAT team to Argentina to rescue us, but we had already escaped! By their reasoning, we were at fault for not advising the CIA sooner of our escape! Paul explained how this had been impossible without giving away our position to Argentina, thus risking recapture, but that we were deeply appreciative of the effort and sorry for the inconvenience we had caused.

As Paul would remark to me later, "This is typical Washington mentality! But remember, Will, we must keep our opinions to ourselves and be polite. Actually, our kidnapping may have awakened the president to the fact that if my colleagues and I have such valuable knowledge that another nation was willing to STEAL it, then maybe they should pay attention to us. This may be our first real opportunity to change some laws in the US! I expect a lot of good may come about because of what we have gone through." Wow! I had never thought about it that way. That made us heroes of sorts!

Well, the Atlantic Ocean whizzed by underneath us so fast compared to the Norse Princess, that I was taken by surprise when we were asked to fasten our seatbelts and prepare for landing. I had been invited to find a book to read in the small library, but had gotten no farther than a few pages. All I could think of was telling Sara about my adventures and finding Mom in some hospital, all smiling and well. As Paul pointed out, we were traveling with the sun, so it was still daytime when we touched down.

After landing we were taken by an electric limo to a CIA office where we gave a detailed account of our kidnapping and escape, (our debriefing), and what, if anything, we might have revealed to the Argentines. Next came a "photo-op" with the president. I got a pat on the head and a handshake from the president and Paul answered a few questions as the press took our pictures. Then we went to the president's office, which was oval just like his old one, they said. Paul and Dr. Gucci did most of the talking while the president and his aides took notes and asked questions. The substance of the conversation was largely over my head, but I shall never forget the immense feeling of pride that I felt for Paul, watching as he explained technical matters to the President of the United States.

This discussion went on for over an hour, after which we went to a hotel, and sat down to dinner with several scientists, all apparently old friends of Paul. Again I was fascinated to listen in on their conversation. This time Dr. Gucci and Pedro were much more involved, talking about tectonic plate movement, etc. That night I shared a room with Paul and before going to sleep, he told me that the president now seemed genuinely interested in pursuing the measures that he and his colleagues were recommending. "Things are looking hopeful for Mother Earth, Will. Now, about your mom, tomorrow we start looking for her!" he said.

I slept well that night.

FEBRUARY 8, 2049
SARA'S ACCOUNT

It had been six days since Mona got the radio message from Paul that Will and he were safe in Europe. There must have been some reason for not disclosing in which country. Mona said that they would surely find safe passage from there to the U.S.; it's just a question of when.

The story about Mom was a different matter. Mona had been in radio contact with every hospital on her list. It was a pretty exhaustive list, but there were numerous small clinics that, in those chaotic times, were in no national registry. I was thankful that she had received help; at least Kate's note sounded hopeful on that point, but where?

I found that keeping busy was the best thing for my spirits. I had become a baby sitter and general all-round helper at the Crow's Nest Nursery School, so that one of the women could help in the farm work. I got paid in love and I loved it!

On this day, at about ten AM, I was outside with the children, before the sun got too hot, when I looked up to see Mona riding pell-mell toward me on her bicycle, known as the "Crow's Nest High Speed Transit System." When she skidded to a stop she said she had just gotten word that Will, Paul, Dr. Gucci, whom she knew, and some other scientist had arrived in Washington on the president's own plane, <u>Air Force One</u>. They were going to be there for a few days, maybe a week, at the invitation of the National Science Foundation, and Paul would address Congress tomorrow! "Finally the powers-that-be are listening to what Paul has to tell them!" said Mona, all out of breath from excitement.

They had discussed the situation about Mom, she said, and Paul would tap into the resources of the government to find her. The FBI could find anyone, she said. Hey! After that conversation the day just flew by!

FEBRUARY 18, 2049
NEW WASHINGTON

We had been in New Washington for over ten days and up to then we had not found Mom. Paul said we must be patient, so I must be. So many things had happened that it seemed like a blur. I guess Paul was considered quite important now, because they assigned a pretty young woman to be my guide, my bodyguard really, because she carried a gun on her hip. I think they were afraid that I might be kidnapped again. Every place I wanted to go she took me, except the bathroom, of course. She sat by my side when Paul addressed Congress and took me to dinner: no charge. Actually, she was really good looking and a good conversationalist, besides. If I had been twenty instead of eleven, I would have liked to be her boyfriend. I told her about all the things that had happened to me and she seemed really impressed. It was nice to have someone who wanted to hear about my adventures.

Pedro and Dr. Gucci had returned to La Paz, Bolivia, the day before. They left on a Bolivian military jet with plenty of soldiers to protect them. I hated to see Pedro go; we had been through so much together. It was Pedro who saved us all in Argentina at great risk to himself. He was a true hero. We had so much fun too, in Italy, visiting the little towns and climbing the hills together. At the airport we promised to keep in touch and I am happy to say that over the years we actually did.

There was much to keep me occupied in Washington, and I did enjoy it, but one overriding thing put a damper on it all. Mom was lost. There were thousands of places she might be, and so far, even the FBI couldn't locate her. It even made me feel guilty to be having fun with my pretty guardian.

It was now the evening of the eighteenth of February. Paul and I sat alone in the hotel restaurant this evening, or as alone as we could be, since the room was crowded with diners and the FBI was in the room too, keeping us safe. My guardian had been dismissed for the day. We were talking about the events of the past week, things I had seen, some highlights of Paul's progress, and when we should return to the Crow's Nest. I was glad to have Paul to myself for a change, because I needed his warmth and attention. I was depressed and Paul was doing his best to cheer me up.

Our table was close to the salad bar so people were constantly brushing past us. Suddenly I heard a man's voice say, "Hi. Do you mind if we join you?"

I looked up from my plate to see a tall man beside our table, and my immediate reaction was to think, "Oh no!

Not another one of Paul's friends to talk about the environment! This was MY evening with Paul!" Fortunately, those words never left my mouth. I glanced at Paul and noted a distinctly puzzled look on his face. He was slowly rising from his chair, when the man reached for Paul's hand and said, "John Anchor, Will's Uncle John."

It took me a second to react, but Paul was saying, "McMaster, Paul McMaster. How wonderful, how incredible! How did you find us? Will, wake up! Look who's here!"

Well, I came to pretty fast. Uncle John was a name to me, not a face; I'm not sure I'd ever met him or seen his photograph. I was standing now, shaking his hand. It was only then that I came out of my daze and saw Aunt Kate standing next to him, looking for all the world as if she would burst! "Aunt Kate!" I screamed, and ran into her arms. The FBI men, ever vigilant, leapt to their feet, as well as a few of the dinner patrons. I should not have been so loud, but I couldn't help myself!

After the initial flurry of activity, and after the waiter had cleaned up the milk I had spilled, they did indeed join us at the table. They ordered dinner and we ordered desert.

First and foremost, I found out that Mom was recuperating comfortably at a doctor's clinic in Maine. She had had surgery and would be there for at least another month. The doctor's name was Moses and having read a bit of the Bible, I imagined exactly what he would look like.

Uncle John, an attorney and my dad's brother, had discovered that Dad was dead from a legal document he had received from Southern Power, the company that owned the Holondorf plant, which Dad had operated. Upon discovering this, he had tried several times to contact Mom, but to no avail. He had a hunch that she might be stranded there, so he had hired the services of a friend and his yacht to check out the situation in New Orleans. Well, the hunch paid off. There was Mom and Kate just "a-sittin an a-waitin" for him. Mom had said emphatically that John's so-called "hunch" was God telling him to get a move on.

We found out that John had practiced law in New York City for years, but after that awful storm, Zandra, had left his office in tatters, he moved to his summer home in Maine, which was near the ocean, but on high ground. Here in a tiny self-sufficient community, that sounded a bit like Paul's, he had found happiness, especially after having met Kate, that is! Here Kate, who was just bubbling over, picked up the conversation. From the moment they met they were in love, she said. They were engaged now, with Mom's blessing, and just looking for the ideal place to tie the knot, she said.

My turn came next. With the help of their questions, the tale of how Sara and I found the Crow's Nest and how Paul had taken us in as if we were his own children, all came tumbling out. Then the kidnapping! Here Paul said he wanted a turn to talk. Well his version was not as exciting as mine would have been, but he got all the basic facts right. Then he said, "But tell me. How on earth did you two find us?"

"With great difficulty!" said Kate. "Just by luck I saw the TV photo-op you had with the president and I recognized Will, despite the fact that they said he was your son. Will, I would recognize anywhere!" I wasn't sure that was a compliment, but I let it pass. Then she went on: "John's little community is isolated, no phone or radio hams. You want to contact someone far away? Try the next town, maybe, or better still the next. It fulfills the old Maine comment, 'You caint get theah from heah,' 'cause you really can't!"

Here John broke in, "Well, it isn't that bad, Kate. You weren't communicating so well in New Orleans, as I recall." I noted that they were both smiling. Then he continued, "As you probably know, Paul, the governor of Maine, several years ago, had ordered all the Holondorf plants closed, upstaging the US government, but virtually eliminating electricity in the state. Result: people have ignored the law against burning things and have gone back to windmills and solar panels, wherever they could find them.

"Anyway, since my electric car wasn't suitable for long trips, with so few places to recharge it, we decided to fire up my old gas engine Miata, fill it with all the fuel we could find and head toward Washington. We did pretty well too, despite the washed-out bridges and new lakes that didn't appear on the map. The Miata sputtered to a stop in the Pennsylvania Dutch country, right in front of an Amish farm. We pushed my baby into the farmer's barnyard and traded my wheels for a taxi ride into Washington, New Washington to be correct, in one of his horse-drawn buggies. Here in Washington, we looked up the press corps and on the promise of an exclusive interview, they led us here. They are waiting in the lobby, by the way, but the farmer said he had to get back home to do the chores."

"Well, then we better get it over with," said Paul. John insisted on paying the bill and off we went to the lobby. This time the interview was more like a TV mini-series. Paul said that although he had been previously married, a widower, he had no children of his own so having Sara and me arrive in his life was like the answer to a dream. Each of us gave our story for the record, answering the interviewer's questions. I suspect this was the seed planted in my mind that eventually gave rise to this book.

While Paul conferred with the FBI and John checked into the hotel, Kate put her arms around me and held me close. "Now I want to see Sara!" she whispered.

FEBRUARY 19, 2049
SARA'S ACCOUNT

When I walked into the kitchen this morning I could tell from Mona's face that she had good news. She told me about Mom and how she got to a surgeon in Maine, a Dr. Moses, and was operated on and was recuperating just fine. She told me how it was Uncle John who had rescued them. I wondered why Kate had not included this bit of information in her note, but maybe she had never met him. (I must have been pretty small, but I recall Uncle John visiting us and giving me a doll.)

Then Mona revealed the best news of all. A chopper would arrive within the hour, bringing Will, Paul, Aunt Kate and Uncle John! We had company coming! Mona would stay at the house and spruce things up; I was to take the bike to the village and let everyone know, especially Tom, so he might change his schedule and bake bread today.

I had no more than arrived at Tom, the baker's door, when I heard the sound of the chopper. This time the plop-plop-plop was no longer terrifying; it was more like sweet music to my ears. I began to deliver my message, but found myself being swept along in a tide of friends all trying to reach the house first! Oh, what wonderful chaos! The chopper stayed just long enough to let folks off and deliver several containers of aircraft fuel. The fuel, as Paul explained later, was an allotment from national reserves due to his improved status in Washington. He could now fly his red plane to Maine to get Mom!

As I think back to that time, the biggest thrill was seeing my little brat brother jump down from the chopper and leap into my arms. It was so good to have him back. We had so much to tell each other, both talking at once. It was great to see Aunt Kate and Paul too, of course.

Then a tall thin man with dark hair approached me. He moved slowly with kind of an animal-like grace, so like Daddy. It was a strange moment for me to feel as if I might be in Daddy's presence again, I may even have called him "Daddy!"

You see, Daddy lost his life saving a child during one of the summer storms. Everyone said that was so, but Daddy's body was never found, so we, Will and I anyway, never completely accepted that he was dead. For months he would come to us in dreams. Will and I compared dreams every morning. Now Uncle John's presence reawakened those feelings in me, and when he took me in his arms I just let it all come out. I just sobbed and sobbed, I had so much bottled up inside of me! In a very real sense, Daddy had returned.

It was then that I remembered the letter that Mom had asked us to mail, the letter to John Anchor, Esq.. I ran to my room and brought it to him, along with Mom's memoir. "Thank you," he said. "The mail service is still working! Actually, your mother told me what it said. I'll save it to read tomorrow. The memoir should go back to your mother, because she will have a lot more she'll want to add to it, I'm sure."

Well, it was one glorious day in every way. The entire village of Crow's Nest had a spur-of-the-moment open house. It was a sunny winter day, about 70 degrees Fahrenheit. The vegetable garden was a showpiece of farming skill. This was the best season of the year; summer was unbearably hot. (John pointed out that Maine was the place to be in summer.)

When John saw the village he was so excited by the design of the buildings, the igloos, that he stayed down there for some time studying the details and discussing them with Paul. He was thinking of doing something similar in Maine, he said.

Another thing that people needed in Maine was some better means of generating electricity. John said he was fortunate to have a windmill, but more than half of the people had nothing. Some had solar cells, like the ones that covered Paul's barn roof. Another device, generally referred to as a solar generator, had been around for decades, but was costly and inefficient. All these methods were reliable, but hard to obtain. Then Paul showed us an experimental device, a promising invention of Mona's that they were testing. Mona's prototype used an entirely different process than other generators available on the market, utilized common materials, and would be less costly to make. Paul said she had a few more kinks to work out before she was ready to go public, however. She kept that behind the barn.

For Kate, it was the abundance of flowers that excited her most. Will had gone off with the men in the village and I had gravitated to Aunt Kate and Mona at Paul's house. Those two hit it off like old bosom buddies. Finally I got the impression that they were keeping a secret from me so I said so point blank. Then Kate, looking a bit sheepish, told me that she and Uncle John were engaged to get married, and they were not sure if I would like that idea. Of course I liked it, why shouldn't I? I don't know why grown-ups sometimes find it hard to talk to children. As I recall, I walked off in a huff! I just hated being excluded from a conversation.

Well, after I'd simmered down, and they had apologized for treating me as a child (I was thirteen, for gosh sakes!) we got down to some serious girl-talk, speculating on a spring wedding there on the terrace garden behind Paul's house. Kate said she and John were planning to make their home in Maine, since it is cooler and has a nice view of the ocean.

Thus the day progressed in visiting, dining and telling about our adventures for all who were willing to listen. Paul and Mona spent several hours discussing the conditions in Argentina and Paul's meetings in Italy and in Washington. Overall, Paul said, the world situation looked hopeful since countries were beginning to realize the changes they must make and the urgency of taking immediate action. His speech to the US Congress was well received and the President was finally on board. "Took a kidnapping to do it. I guess I owe a debt of thanks to Argentina," he said, with a chuckle.

That evening, sitting under the stars, with Uncle John on one side and Will on the other, and Snowball taking turns on our laps, was the perfect ending for a perfect day. John explained more completely what Mom had been suffering from, and the doctor's assurance that the operation had not only saved her life, but that she could expect to have a long healthy life from here on. She must have another month of complete rest, however, in order to recuperate properly before trying to travel. That was so comforting to hear and I appreciated the fact that John trusted us kids with the facts, instead of some gold-plated version. Children that are shielded from the truth are forced to guess at it, often with nightmarish results.

We all sat up late on this evening and when I finally turned in, with Snowball of course, I slept like a rock.

FEBRUARY 20–MARCH 3, 2049
THE CROWS NEST

What a busy time this was! Paul and John worked on over-hauling the red airplane in the barn for the trip to Maine to get Mom. It had been in "mothballs" for years, according to Paul. Mice had nested inside it, chewing on wires and hoses, so everything needed careful inspection. I heard Paul and John joking about the fact that Paul had been in "moth-balls" too and could he still remember how to fly. "It's like riding a bicycle, John, It will all come back to me when I see the ground rushing toward me!" Paul said laughingly.

Aunt Kate busied herself on two fronts, preparing a bed-room for Mom and helping in the small clinic run by Mildred, "the nurse." The Crow's Nest had no doctor so Kate's experience was very welcome. Sara and I helped where we were needed; schooling was postponed until later.

The trip to Maine was planned as follows: John, Paul and Sara would go in the plane and return with Mom. (The plane could only hold four people.) Sometime after Mom's return, Kate and John would be married at The Crow's Nest. Then Paul and I would take the newly-weds to Maine where they wanted to live, and Paul and I would fly back. Paul said that he would stop in New Washington, which is about half way, to refuel using the fuel reserves he had been promised.

Mona had managed to contact Dr. Moses in Maine by radio. Mom was now up and about and anxious to travel so the trip was planned for March 4th if the weather permitted. The tiny airport near the clinic would be expecting them, and provided their GPS location.

MARCH 4, 2049
FLYING
SARA'S ACCOUNT

On the morning of March 4th the weather at The Crow's Nest was clear and in Washington as well, but Maine was not answering our call. Paul showed me the windsock on top of the barn that showed him the direction of the wind. He said that you always take off and land into the wind. The landing strip was a long grassy area beginning at the barn and extending almost to the end of the island. The goats often grazed there, but today they were firmly locked away in their shed, out of harm's way.

Aunt Kate and Mona made sure I was wearing the right kind of clothes, especially, a warm jacket because it gets cold up in the sky and in Maine. Will had told me how cold he got in the helicopter, but I figured it was because he was scared. Paul and Uncle John sat up front, while I sat behind them. After we got all settled, seat belts fastened, we slowly taxied to the end of the runway furthest from the barn. There he tested the engine with the brakes on for about a minute. Finally, with a great roar, we began to roll faster and faster until we lifted off the ground and I saw the barn and all the rest of The Crow's Nest pass beneath us. We were on our way!

The view from up there was breathtaking to say the least. We had taken off heading south and we were now turning to the north. From here I had a view of the expanse of water that Will and I had traveled over in the canoe. It was huge! To myself I murmured, "I know what Mom would say about who helped us."

I was soon very glad to have the warm jacket. Will was right; it was cold up there. Looking down I could see mountains beneath us, the lines of roads and often the speck of a car or truck. Towns stood out clearly and people too, like black pepper sprinkled on the landscape. They were looking up at us, just as I was looking down at them. It was so wild and weird—this, my first look down on the Earth. Far off to the right, the east, I could see the shimmer of water at times, a sure sign of flooded towns. There was so much to see out the window and yet the hypnotic drone of the engine was putting me to sleep. I had my doll with me (Snowball wasn't allowed to come) so I let myself be a little girl again and closed my eyes. Uncle John must have looked at me about then because I heard him say to Paul, "She's asleep back there." I didn't say a word.

Well, that is exactly what I did. I fell asleep and did not wake up until I felt the bump as we landed in New Washington Airport. Paul had to taxi a long distance on tarmac, following yellow painted lanes until we got to a place to park and refuel. To me it looked like a very busy place, but Paul said it was practically deserted. Inside the terminal there was a ladies restroom, (another "first" for me), and a lunch counter where we ate.

We were nearly done eating when suddenly a young man in a black suit and tie rushed up to Paul, saying how glad he was to see Paul (he called him Dr. McMaster) and he hadn't realized that he was "in town" and could he please come to a very important meeting, because the future of some bill was hanging in the balance. Paul's reaction was interesting. He said, "Sorry, Joe, this one you have to handle yourself, because I'm on a tight schedule and am leaving ASAP." With that he jumped up saying, "Come on Sara, John, we have a long road ahead," and with the man, Joe, still trying to get a word in, we returned to the plane.

The plane had been refueled so I assumed that we would take off and continue our trip. Instead, we taxied to an area where several other small planes were parked and tied down. Paul did the same. Paul was still muttering about Joe and all the other "hangers on" who were unwilling or unable to stand on their own two feet, when by a tug on his arm, I got his attention. "I don't want to be a 'hangers on,' but what are we doing?"

"Oh Sara, I'm sorry! I get so tied up in my own thoughts that I forget the people that mean the most to me. You're no 'hangers on'. You and Will are like family to me and I think of you as my children, children my wife and I never managed to have." Paul had kneeled in front of me as he said this, so that we were face-to-face. "Am I forgiven?" he said.

My response was to fling my arms about his neck and whisper, "Yes!"

With that he explained that Maine appeared to be having heavy weather of some kind, maybe even snow, since it was winter. John agreed that Maine often had ice and snow, despite the effects of global warming. We would stay at a motel for the night and check the weather report in the morning. We had a long flight ahead of us, over a thousand miles and it was essential to arrive in daylight. John asked Paul if his plane had de-icing equipment, but I didn't hear his answer.

It was mid-afternoon when we settled in our rooms. They were nice and clean, but both rooms smelled strongly of tobacco. There was a TV and a selection of movies, with a slot for coins. Paul looked over the list and picked one that he said was suitable called "Black Beauty" and we all watched it together. When it was done I wanted to see it again! Paul thought that was funny, but put in the additional coins and let me watch it anyway.

We had supper in a restaurant after that, but I was still so wrapped up in my movie I don't remember much about the meal. Soon I was in bed and that lovely horse was there in my dreams as well.

MARCH 5–7, 2049
NEW WASHINGTON
SARA'S ACCOUNT

The next day, it was raining, at least where we were, in New Washington, Virginia. Paul said the rain here was not keeping us from flying, but it was reported that Maine was getting freezing rain, and that was serious stuff. We were staying here to wait it out, but to keep us from getting bored, he and John had located a book store and bought a book for each of us: <u>Black Beauty</u> by Anna Sewell for me, <u>War and Peace</u> by Leo Tolstoy for Paul. He said it was a classic that he had never found time to read. Uncle John had a book too, but I forget the name.

Paul said he preferred to "lay low," hoping that Joe, and others like him, would not find him and draw him into the political bickering that he hated. Paul was a scientist, not a politician.

For my part I couldn't have been happier. The book, <u>Black Beauty</u>, was even better than the movie, and it was my very own! It was so nice to have all of us reading together in the lounge, sipping tea and coffee, listening to soft music and the beat of rain on the huge windows. I loved feeling so snug and safe inside.

After three days of this, we were becoming edgy, however, and anxious to go. On the evening of March 7th, Paul said the weather up north had broken, and we were to get an early start in the morning. This time I would really see Mom; I was so excited I could hardly sleep that night.

MARCH 8, 2049—
JAFFREY, NH
SARA'S ACCOUNT

It was still dark when we walked out to the plane and stowed our luggage. Fortunately for us, the small restaurant at the motel catered to early risers, so we were able to enjoy a good breakfast before taking off. Back at the plane again, Paul did his preflight checks, with John and me closely watching the procedure. Some day, I thought, maybe I would be a pilot too.

This time, Paul got permission from the tower by radio before taking off. There were several runways and Paul explained that we were being directed to the one where we could take off into the wind. After we were high in the air, we slowly tuned to the northeast. I watched the scenery slowly unfold beneath us for awhile, but soon went back to my book for a second reading. The cabin of the plane was heated, but I was glad to have the warmth of the new sweater that Uncle John had bought me in New Washington, to "keep me warm in Maine."

I noticed that Paul was flying closer to the ground this time, just under the clouds. We had a "low ceiling", he said, and I could detect a note of concern in his voice. As the hours rolled by, the clouds became lower and darker, and it was only 2 PM by my watch, when I heard John shout, "I see an airport! Over there, to the right! What do you think?"

Paul must have agreed, because we flew in that direction. Coming in low over the field, we made a wide slow turn, gently landed, and taxied up to the terminal. There were no signs of people anywhere, no planes, no lights; it was ghostly quiet when the engine stopped! Then I noticed high weeds growing in what was once a flowerbed. Then Paul said, "Guess they don't have curb service," at which both men laughed. I didn't get the joke and the sudden cessation of our trip frightened me. I didn't understand.

I'm sure I was crying a little when I blurted out angrily, "Why did we stop and why here of all places? I want to see Mom!"

Paul and John turned to face me then and explained how we were forced to land because of the low cloud ceiling, which we had to stay under, since we did not have instruments needed to safely fly through clouds. Besides that, we were getting close to the White Mountains, which were too high to fly over anyway. Those, we would fly between, but only with clear weather to see by. "It's a bit like canoeing, Sara. You go when the conditions are safe and stay holed up if they aren't," said Paul. "Now let's see if we can make ourselves comfortable in that deserted terminal."

After tying the plane down to loops in the paving, we walked toward the building. A sign on the wall, and also painted in huge letters on the roof, told us we were at Jaffrey, NH. When we reached the door, to my surprise, I read another sign hanging there. We were welcome, it read, to stay as long as we wished. There was firewood for the stove, but we were to replace what we used for the next visitor. We were to leave the terminal as we found it!

The door was unlocked and the small lobby was clean and neat. There was a large braided rug on the floor and a variety of comfortable furniture, all in decent condition. The stove was a large pot bellied monster that dominated the center of the room, with a large wood box nearby, filled to overflowing. I went into the bathroom, which had a skylight for light and a composting toilet of the kind that Paul used at the Crow's Nest. There was a sink, but the water was turned off. (Later we found an old-fashioned pitcher pump behind the terminal. Pumping took a while, but when the water began flowing it was clear, cold, and plentiful.)

When I returned to the main area, John already had a small fire started and Paul was bringing in our sleeping bags and gear. There was no electricity, but several kerosene lamps stood ready for use. They had considered everything, and I felt humbled after my previous grumbling. Paul said we had several days supply of food, and since we had skipped lunch, John, with a little help from me, soon had a meal on the table.

That evening we all got a good look at Paul's map, which pinpointed our location and the route we would follow, as soon as conditions were safe. After a wonderful evening of swapping stories and singing songs, we turned in early. I stretched out on one of the couches and slept like a log.

MARCH 9, 2049— MAINE SARA'S ACCOUNT

When I opened my eyes the following morning, sun was streaming through the windows. It was a clear crisp day, perfect for flying! I quickly dressed and went outside to breathe in the cool fresh air, so different from the air in New Orleans. I walked around the terminal. Tall handsome trees surrounded the airport runway. I ran to stand under their branches, watching the squirrels and birds scurry away, I felt the grandeur of nature, the thrill of life as seldom before! I was going to see Mom! I was pulled from my reverie by a loud whistle, and saw Paul waving me back. We were having pancakes and they were ready to eat! What a great way to start a day!

After cleaning up and replenishing the firewood, which we cut from fallen branches in the woods, we signed our names in the guest book and left. The most recent entry in the book was "Dr. B. K. Thompson," about four months prior, an old acquaintance of Paul's, from his "wild days." I could not get Paul to elaborate on that, except to say, laughingly, "Hope we don't meet him." (Later I was to learn that he was a paid lobbyist for the Holondorf Power Consortium, a naysayer who claimed Paul was wrong, and that Holondorf should continue operating).

Soon we were back in the air and now the scenery was so glorious that I put my book aside. John, holding the map, pointed out Lake Winnipesauke, then Mount Washington, on our left, it's top lost in the clouds above us. The coast of the Atlantic Ocean was just visible to our right.

The further we went the closer we came to the ocean. I was so used to seeing vast expanses of dirty water, that the Atlantic seemed to be pristine, from the air, at least. The shoreline was rocky and I could see white foam where the waves broke against them. Paul and John were busy now with the GPS, zeroing in on the airport.

After maybe half an hour, the field came into view, a bright orange windsock tilted by the wind to show its direction and approximate force. First Paul over-flew the field to signal our arrival, then returned and landed. As we taxied up to the tiny terminal building, a small electric car came whizzing up to meet us. "That'll be Andrew," said John.

Out stepped a tall heavily bearded man, wearing a plaid shirt and jeans. As soon as the propeller stopped he was at our door, offering his hand to Paul. "Moses," he said.

Paul replied, "So glad to meet you, doctor! I'm Paul McMaster. The weather up here is great!" Then John introduced me and I said something similar. As we gathered our gear from the plane I noticed that John and Andrew Moses had stepped aside and began slapping each other on the back as if they were sharing a joke.

Andrew's electric car was small, but somehow we all fit in. We would go directly to the clinic to get Mom, and his wife, and then we were all to go to a seafood restaurant for lunch. "Sounds wonderful, doctor," said Paul. On the way they talked about the ban placed on Holondorf plants in the state of Maine, and emergence of solar cells and windmills, and safe methods that were in the works, such as Mona's invention.

It was usually fun to listen to Paul discuss scientific matters, but today my whole being was centered on Mom. FINALLY we reached the clinic, and as soon as the car stopped moving I leapt out and ran pell-mell for the entrance. I was approaching the door when it opened wide. There before me was Mom, my own dear Mom, nicely dressed and looking as pretty as a picture. I ran to her immediately and let myself be smothered in her arms. Right beside her stood a small blond headed woman in pigtails, sweatshirt and jeans, the doctor's wife I guessed. Mom said, "Sara, I want you to meet Dr. Moses!"

"I already met him, Mom," I said.

With that, the small woman beside her said something like, "Oh! Andrew! You didn't!" and just doubled over with laughter, leaving me thoroughly puzzled. About then Andrew stepped forward, his face rather red, and confessed that he and John were having a little fun with us. He said that he was indeed married to this little pig-tailed woman, but despite the fact that he resembled Moses from the Bible, it was his wife Dr. Elizabeth Moses, who was the doctor and deserved all the credit. Then he said, "When Paul referred to me as 'Doctor' back at the plane, I couldn't help myself".

Now, hugging her husband, Dr Moses told us "for the record" that Andrew was the builder, plumber, electrician and all round handyman who built the clinic, drove the ambulance, helped with nursing, and, as full time comedian, kept everyone in a good mood.

Now it was my turn to introduce Paul, who was kind of standing back taking it all in. "Mom," I said, "This is Paul and he's the greatest!"

"I kind of gathered that." she replied, and extending her hand, "I'm Marie Anchor and I am so very grateful for all you have done for my children, and now for me. You have united our family; no, more than that, you have saved us."

I had never seen Paul at a loss for words, but now he seemed rather overwhelmed. He stood there holding Mom's hand, murmuring something about how much Will and I meant to him and how glad he was to meet her. Then after an embarrassingly long time, Paul turned his attention to Dr. Moses and thanked her profusely for her work in making Mom whole.

Then I heard Andrew's booming voice say, "Isn't anyone hungry? Let's go. I'll take Marie, Sara and Paul on the first load and come back for John and my sweetie in the second load, OK?" So off we went, Mom and I snuggled in the rear, Andrew and Paul up front.

The restaurant was a modest little building perched on a high bluff overlooking the ocean. We were shown to a table with a grand view of the breakers crashing against the rocky shore, but it seemed very clear that Mom and Paul were much more interested in each other. I was beginning to suspect something.

By the time Andrew returned with Uncle John and Dr. Moses, (who insisted we call her Liz), Paul and Mom had covered just about every subject on earth, with no end in sight! Finally, with all six of us at the table, and the food ordered, they came out of isolation and joined the group in conversation. Don't get me wrong, I was very fond of Paul, but as I sat there almost unnoticed, I wanted Mom's attention and I wasn't getting it. (Remember, I was only thirteen.)

Then, suddenly, Mom looked at me, and said, "Oh Sara, I've missed you so! Tell me about how you found this man." Well, now that I finally had my turn, I gave a capsule rendition of our canoe trip and the wonderful experience of finding the Crow's Nest. Everyone gave me their full attention now, and asked me questions, so that I felt like a member of the party. In no time my petulant feelings had melted away leaving me with fine memories of that fabulous luncheon party, with so many great stories to hear, the delicious food, the thrilling boom of the breakers and, most of all, the sense of camaraderie we shared. We were survivors in a world gone mad.

It was mid-afternoon when we finished lunch and stepped from the restaurant. Paul and Mom said they wanted to explore a path that led down closer to the ocean. I started to follow them, when John beckoned to me, and whispered in my ear, "I think they want to be alone for awhile. Since the car only holds four, let's leave them and do a little exploring ourselves." Then shouting to Paul, "We'll pick you up in an hour."

This time Liz drove, I sat up front beside her, and the two men managed to squeeze into the rear seats. As we drove along a narrow road, high above the rocky shoreline, I looked at the view, but my thoughts were centered on Mom and Paul. Andrew called my attention to the fact that almost every house had a windmill beside it, and many had solar panels on the roof. He was starting to explain about the Holondorf plants being closed in Maine, when Liz interrupted him and said, "I'm not sure that power genera-tion is at the center of Sara's interest just now. I bet she's thinking what I'm thinking. I'm thinking that Marie and Paul are more than just a little interested in each other, and Sara finds this a bit scary, having only recently lost her dad. I've heard a lot about your dad, Sara, he was a wonderful man and maybe it seems as if Paul is suddenly just march-ing in and trying to take his place. That's a very scary thought since no one will ever, ever take your dad's place in your heart." She had stopped the car at an overlook. The view was beautiful, but I could barely see it through my tears. Liz knew just what I'd been thinking!

Liz turned off the motor now and took my hand in hers. I began blubbering something about being "sorry" and she continued, saying how change was hard. Andrew and John were very quiet in the back seat. Then she talked about how she was so lucky to have met Andrew, after being a "bachelor" girl for so long. Then she said that even John, after all the times she had tried to fix him up with a nice woman, was beginning to act like a normal human being, having proposed to Aunt Kate. (I could see where she was going, and that is where she went). Both Mom and Paul needed and deserved someone to love. This did not infer that Mom no longer loved Dad, or Paul, his former wife. We should be happy for them if they find happiness together. "And speaking of love," she said, "I'm pretty darn fond of the whole bunch of you folks!"

Well, this was a pretty "big pill" that the doctor had handed me, but as we sat there quietly saying nothing, I began to see things differently. Liz was a doctor of the mind as well as the body and when Andrew said, "Can we laugh yet?" that's exactly what we did.

"Thanks," I said.

"You're welcome," said Liz, "You'll get my bill in the mail."

With that Liz switched on the motor and our little car, with barely a sound, went purring down the road. "John, may I charge up at your place? The battery won't go much farther than that," said Liz.

"Of course," he replied, "and while it's charging I can show Sara where I live. Kate loves it too."

At that point Andrew spoke up, "You're right John, you have a beautiful home and a great view of the ocean. I suspect that is why Kate agreed to marry you!"

"Now, now, be nice," said Liz. By this time we were all laughing; John most of all.

Suddenly the car entered a grove of tall pines, emerging into a clearing. There sat a low ranch house and beyond it an unobstructed view of the Atlantic Ocean. A windmill stood to one side, spinning wildly.

As soon as the car was plugged in, John took me on a tour of his home. A neighbor had been watching over it during his absence, he said, and feeding his dog. The dog, a black Lab, met us the instant we opened the door. Oh my! What a greeting I got! It was love at first sight. I don't remember too much about the house except the view. It was much smaller than Paul's, having been built recently in a time of shortages, but the walls were thick for strength and insulation. Large windows faced south to collect warmth in winter and had a deep protective overhang to give shade in the summer.

When the car was charged, Liz and Andrew rushed back to get Mom and Paul, since their hour was almost over. We were to be John's guests that evening so the two of us started supper preparations. Food preparation, it turned out, was John's forte. By the time the car returned, a delicious supper was already underway, and a crackling fire burned in the fireplace. It was cold outside now, the sun low in the sky, but it was delightful indoors.

Mom came through the door first, her face rosy and her eyes sparkling. She looked so healthy and so happy. I led her to a comfortable chair by the fire, then sat by her legs on the floor with the Lab, Shadow by name, pressing up against me on the other side. Andrew and Paul were discussing building design (Andrew had built John's house), and Liz went to help John in the kitchen.

It was such a peaceful scene; everything felt so right. The petty feelings of jealousy I had felt earlier were completely banished; now the sense of having both Mom and Paul, the sense of family, seemed to completely fill the room. If only Will had been there too, to make it complete!

Well, I forget what John and Liz made for supper, but I'm sure it was good. We sat up late by the fire that night, long after Liz and Andrew went home, telling stories, and singing to the accompaniment of John's guitar. It was magical, and when we finally turned in, I slept with Mom in the guest room bed. It had been quite a day!

MARCH 10, 2049—
HOMECOMING
SARA'S ACCOUNT

The next morning I awoke to the sight of the sun breaking on the sparkling and endless ocean. Mom awoke at the same time and we sat there on the edge of the bed, looking at it, arms about each other, covers wrapped over our shoulders. This time we talked, really talked. I told her about the jealous feelings I had felt yesterday, and how Liz had set me straight. I told her that now I just prayed that she would marry Paul so we would all be together, forever and ever.

Mom said I was getting a little into never-never land. She said she was indeed very attracted to Paul, and he to her, apparently. Marriage, however, was not on the table, certainly not yet. Why, they had only just met, for gosh sakes! Maybe in a few more months, but, only maybe. "Well, I do like him a lot, but I mustn't think like that. It's too soon after Daddy, Sara, too soon!" she murmured. She was half crying, half laughing and soon we were both going at it. Mom was in love and we both knew it. I, for one, was delighted!

At breakfast that morning, Paul looked happier than I had ever seen him look. The weather between Maine and New Washington was good for flying, he reported, but did we want to leave yet? It was up to me to decide, he said.

My response, "Let's go HOME!"

With that Shadow barked "Woof!"

"Sorry, Shadow, you're outnumbered," said John. "I'll buzz Andrew to let them know we're going today. I'll take my four-seater to the airport also and Andrew can bring it home. Time to pack up."

Well, after all the hugs, and good wishes, the preflight checks and the map reading, our little red plane took off with Paul and John up front and Mom and I behind them. We were going to the Crow's Nest, the place that I now thought of, as "home" and I couldn't wait to show it off to Mom.

MARCH 7–11, 2049
THE CROWS NEST

Life at the Crow's Nest had settled into a pleasant routine since Paul and my sister left to get Mom. Mona worked in Paul's house and Aunt Kate spent her time with the nurse, Mildred, teaching each other things they had learned over the years. I spent part of the day baby-sitting for Anne (Anne with an "e") and the rest at school. To most people school means a big building with lots of classrooms. Not here. Each class was in a separate igloo, taught by the person who lived there. Paul taught science and engineering at his house, when he was home; now Mona did it. My classes were in the village, with ten other kids learning math, languages and agriculture. I was starting to find friends my own age.

It was five o'clock, school was over, and I was just rounding the corner of the barn on my way home, when I heard the low rumble of a plane. Paul was not expected for several days, but I foolishly assumed that it was he. I raced to the far corner of the barn just in time to see a silver twin-prop airplane taxi to a stop almost beside me. Remembering, all too well, my recent kidnapping, I ran screaming for the house.

Mona met me at the door, took me in her arms and told me it was nothing to be afraid of. She knew this "old buzzard" she said. She said he was a real "bad egg", but not a bit dangerous. I was thoroughly bewildered!

Mona walked right up to the man who stepped out. He was medium height, had snowy white hair and a rather silly looking moustache, also pure white. I hung back a little, but heard all the conversation. She piled right into him, "What do you mean, Bert, scaring the daylights out of my friend here? And what kind of trouble are you here for anyway? Still running interference for Holondorf? Speak up man!"

"I will, Mona my love, if you just shut up long enough for me to speak," he said, laughing. "I came to see Paul anyway, not you. Where is he? And regarding your friend here, I apologize. B.K. Thompson, young fellow."

We shook hands. I was still confused, but gathered they really liked each other, in a way. Mona invited him to the house where they sat in the kitchen, sipping sun tea and talking in a sort of scientific jargon that I barely understood. They disagreed on some things, but seemed united on others. When it was agreed that he could stay for a few days, in order to see Paul, I was really surprised. Who was this guy?

For the next four days, he sat under the trees reading Paul's books, while I went to baby-sit, and to school, and Mona taught engineering to several older students. Just sat there reading Paul's books. It kind of irked me, but I said nothing. Mona and B.K. continued the sort of friendly sarcasm I had heard earlier, and I had no opportunity to question her privately about him.

Finally, on the eleventh, again as I was coming home from school, I heard Paul as he came in low over the barn, then came back to land. I was the first to arrive at the plane, but I was soon joined by a crowd of others, all wanting to welcome Paul and to meet Mom. Well, there she was looking beautifully radiant and pink cheeked. Oh how wonderful she felt in my arms! This time it was I who did the honors, introducing her to everyone in the crowd. (Back then I had a talent for remembering names, a talent I seem to have lost).

Walking now to the house, Mom on one side, Sara on the other, I saw that B.K. was still sitting on a chair under the trees, book in hand. I watched as Paul, with Mona at his side, approached him. B.K. spoke first, "Good book, Paul. One you wrote, I see. I find myself agreeing with you. Are you surprised?"

"He's been here waiting to see you, Paul," said Mona. "He claims he wants to make nice."

Paul said, "Well, you're smart, Bert. When outnumbered, smile and act humble. Good survival tactic. So, what are you really here for?"

That was all I heard of the conversation, because Sara was rushing Mom inside to see the house. That evening

B.K. was invited to supper, after which, he, Mona, John and Paul went into Paul's office and closed the door, not to be seen again until bedtime. Something big was going on and I was being left out of it.

MARCH 12, 2049
THE CROWS NEST

This morning I woke up late, just in time to see B.K. climb into his plane with Paul, John, and Mona standing by, all of them laughing and apparently on the friendliest of terms. When B.K.'s plane was off the ground, they walked slowly to the house talking, even stopping at one point to debate some point they were discussing. Maybe now we would find out what was going on. I planned to ask.

Last night, Sara had told me about what she had found out: that B.K. had been a paid lobbyist for the Holondorf industry, a naysayer, proclaiming that Holondorf was blameless and the sinking of landmasses was due to other causes. From what she heard, Paul had little use for the man.

At breakfast, when we were all seated, I was about to pop the question, when Paul beat me to it. "I'm sure you are wondering what we were doing, getting cozy with Bert

Thompson, the man who came close to being my nemesis a year or so ago. Well, the Holondorf people paid Bert handsomely to take their side, and he let greed buy his soul for years, making Bert a very wealthy man in monetary terms, but a ruined man, as far as his reputation as a scientist is concerned. Well, it seems that old Bert has reached that point where his reputation means more than money. Kind of like Ebenezer Scrooge in Dickens' <u>Christmas Carol</u> finding out that 'mankind WAS his business'."

"Bert and I were classmates back in college," he continued, "There is no question that he is smart, but he is short on scruples. Anyway, he has left the employ of the Holondorf Consortium and is willing to publicly tell the truth, for a change. Then in exchange for our acceptance, he will help promote Mona's invention, the prototype she has sitting out behind the barn. He realizes that her design has tremendous potential to provide the world with safe electricity replacing Holondorf plants. It will take a lot of money, which he has in abundance. He will do serious development of her concept and get it to market in his plant in Pennsylvania, footing the bill. Of course, he sees the potential for making a lot of money off of it some day and at the same time, improving his image. For Mona too, it's a win-win situation." At this, Paul stopped talking to let it all sink in; Mona just sat there smiling.

Up to now, John had said nothing, just sat there nodding his head. Now he said, "Don't worry about Doctor Thompson conveniently forgetting what he has promised. I made up a legally binding contract last night for him to sign. He signed it with witnesses, so if he has a lapse of memory some day, we can help him remember."

Well, it was a lot to absorb all right. I had read The Christmas Carol by Charles Dickens, but I found it hard to imagine B.K. in the roll of Scrooge; he just didn't fit the part. Sara and I sat very quietly thinking about it all, but not Mom. She was full of questions, wanted to go out and see Mona's prototype, the works. So after breakfast we gave her the grand tour of the Crow's Nest. Mona explained her device in detail, while Snowball walked around the edge of it. Then we walked to the village to meet everyone again and to see the igloos. John and Kate had gone off on a walk of their own.

Back at the house we followed a path that took us to an overlook, so Mom could see the expanse of water that Sara and I had paddled across. There was a nice boulder there to sit on so we sat down and Snowball immediately jumped on Mom's lap. The water went to the horizon and Mom just sat there hugging us, tears pouring down her face, and thanking God for guiding us here. We told her some of what we had done, the tree house we had slept in, so many things. Then Mom said she had a very serious question to ask us, and that we must give it a lot of thought before we replied. Then she said softly, "How would you feel if I agreed to marry Paul?"

Sara and I did not have to think very long about that! Before the words left her mouth we were shouting our agreement. I had been secretly hoping for that to happen ever since Paul and I were kidnapped; Sara, I know, felt the same way! We danced around Mom and kissed her.

"Guess I've got my answer," said Mom, all smiles, as we walked slowly to the house.

JUNE 28, 2100
MY BIRTHDAY

Today is my birthday. I, Will Anchor, am sixty-two years old today. It is time I believe, to bring this tale, our odyssey in search of higher ground, to a close. Let me give you some highlights of what happened during the intervening years.

That spring of 2049 seemed to fulfill all our fondest wishes. Mom and Paul were married on a beautiful day under the trees in a double wedding with Aunt Kate and Uncle John. The Crow's Nest's elderly minister, Rev. Angela Smith, came out of retirement to do the honors from her wheelchair. Sara and I carried the rings, being very careful not to get them mixed up. The whole village was there to cheer them on! It was a truly glorious day!

Then, a day or so later, I was privileged to accompany Paul, taking Kate and John to live in Maine. I, too, met the cute pig-tailed woman who had saved Mom's life: Dr. Elizabeth Moses, and her tall bearded husband, Andrew. We dined in the same restaurant that Sara had described to me. She had described it so well that I had a sense of having been there before.

At the airport, before we departed for home, Andrew, said in his booming voice, "Paul, you better teach Will to fly this bird, 'cause I can see a lot of traveling twixt Mississippi and Maine when kids start getting born, an' all that!"

"You're right, Andrew," said Paul, "Ready to fly her home, Son?" Well, I had a lot to learn, but with Paul's guidance over the years, I became a good pilot, and I did indeed ferry our children back and forth many times.

Paul always remained "Paul" to me. "Dad" never quite fit, and Paul understood that very well. Mom was back in her element, teaching school and doing gardening. It was so wonderful to see Mom happy and healthy again. Mom and Paul lived for many contented years together at the Crow's Nest, living well into their nineties.

Sara became a medical doctor and began her career at the Crow's Nest, setting up a badly needed clinic, before moving to Maine. There she was married and has worked for many years as an associate of Dr. Moses. I am so grateful to Sara for the diary she kept as a girl. Without that day-by-day record of events, we might not have been able to write this memoir. I have lived all these years at the Crow's Nest, so I miss my smarty-pants sister very much. The separation makes our occasional visits all the sweeter.

Mona joined B. K. Thompson at his plant in Pennsylvania and earned her doctorate degree while developing her generator in preparation for manufacturing. As many of my readers know, Mona, Dr. Mona L. Greenbaum, went on to win the Nobel Prize for her work with the Thompson Generator, as it is now called. It was the generator, primarily, that ushered in the current wave of prosperity, providing really inexpensive solar power, far more abundantly than the Holondorf plants ever achieved, and with no environmental risk. Scientists tell us that global warming is finally beginning to reverse and the settling of landmasses appears to have ended. Much of this improvement in the environment is traceable to Mona's brilliant work. On a more personal note, Mona never married, but did seem to hit it off with Bert Thompson, who, surprisingly, did turn his life around.

Aunt Kate and Uncle John settled for the rest of their lives in Maine, she as a nurse in Liz's clinic, he with his law practice. John and Andrew experimented with the igloo concept, adapting the design he had seen here at the Crow's Nest for their colder weather in Maine, and eventually building a small community similar to the village here. It is gratifying to note that the idea has caught on elsewhere in the world, especially in earthquake-prone regions, providing safe, inexpensive housing. There is even a company in India that makes thick-walled polystyrene igloos built on floating platforms so that, in flood-prone areas, the house becomes a boat when the monsoon strikes! Now that's good design!

For my part, I never really left the Crow's Nest. After completing basic engineering under Paul's direction, I continued my studies at Cornell University majoring in botany and agriculture. The world became fractured when I was a child; lettuce no longer came from California, apples

from New Zealand. For the most part, all life became localized, more as it was several centuries ago, and in many
ways it has remained so. I see this as a good trend and with
our new knowledge of food and how to produce it, I am
very optimistic about the future for our dear old planet.
Things are gradually getting better.

After my college years I married Amy, my school chum
from the village and we raised our family there, moving
eventually to Paul's house when they needed our help. We
have two fine children, a girl and a boy, named, on Amy's
absolute insistence, Sara and Will!

Now, I must leave you. I am being called to blow out the
candles on my cake!

THE END

978-0-595-47590-2
0-595-47590-6

Made in the USA
Lexington, KY
03 April 2011